TAKE ME, I'M YOURS

Melissa D'Angelo is tired of being the only twenty-four-year-old virgin in Seattle. Before entering medical school, she needs a lover with no strings attached. Harvard Law School graduate Jake Mallory loves women and they love him. But a pregnancy scare with a woman he barely knew birthed a vow of celibacy and a growing need for love, family and commitment. The moment Jake and Melissa meet at a local club, passion ignites. But Melissa can't allow sex to lead to love — and love and family are all Jake wants . . .

Books by Gael Morrison
in the Linford Romance Library:

PASSION OF THE DRUMS
HEART OF A WOMAN
LOVERS NEVER LIE
MEET ME AT MIDNIGHT

GAEL MORRISON

◆

TAKE ME, I'M YOURS

LINFORD
Leicester

First published in Great Britain in 2014

First Linford Edition
published 2016

A catalogue record for this book is available
from the British Library.

ISBN 978–1–4448–2696–8

Published by
F. A. Thorpe (Publishing)
Anstey, Leicestershire

Set by Words & Graphics Ltd.
Anstey, Leicestershire
Printed and bound in Great Britain by
T. J. International Ltd., Padstow, Cornwall

This book is printed on acid-free paper

Dedication

For Cheryl

1

Jake Mallory scowled at the phone on his desk and wished like hell that it would ring. Wished too that the pain drilling its way through his skull would pierce the haze cloaking his brain.

He could blame his mental fog on the Beaujolais Tammy had served the night before, but he knew his lack of clarity hadn't stemmed from drinking wine, but rather from the moment Tammy uttered the words, 'I'm pregnant.'

Jake expelled the air trapped in his throat.

He shouldn't think of Tammy now.

Could think of nothing else.

He had to pull himself together.

He was due in court in two hours.

A soft tap sounded on his office door.

'Come in,' he growled, not shifting his gaze from the phone.

Jenny, his assistant, opened the door.

'Morning, Jake,' she said, as she entered his office.

'Morning,' he grunted.

'Aren't these gorgeous?'

Jenny's question demanded that he look up. Reluctantly, he did so. Immediately wished he hadn't. He winced at the sight of the flowers in Jenny's arms. 'What do you expect me to do with those?'

This wasn't the morning for sunny spring blossoms. He didn't feel sunny, and the day outside wasn't like any spring he'd ever known, especially in Seattle.

It was hot, damn hot. The heat was making him sweat even in the air-conditioned cool of his office. Or maybe it was the flowers Jenny had brought that had started perspiration beading his temples. He couldn't help but equate flowers with a gift for a new mother sitting in a maternity ward holding her baby.

Jake swirled his chair around to face the window and glanced towards the harbor. What he needed was a ticket on one of the cruise ships he could see lining the docks. He could head up to Alaska where the weather was still cold, and where there were fewer women to drive a man mad.

With a sigh, he slowly swung his chair back.

Jenny, who hadn't even bothered to answer his question, was instead placing the flower vase on his desk where her blooms proceeded to droop over his phone.

'Don't put them there,' he commanded.

In answer, she touched a sprig of tiny blossoms. 'My garden's spectacular this year,' she said softly, 'although I didn't grow this baby's breath.'

Jenny had once told him that when women became pregnant all they could see were other women in the same condition. Was his special torture going to be mauve and pink flowers and references to babies wherever he went?

He pushed the vase toward Jenny.

'Take them away.'

Jenny's brows drew together, but she picked up the vase and shifted it to a spot on the window sill. 'What's up?' she asked, giving the flowers a final caress. 'How come you're here so early?'

It hadn't seemed too early when he woke up in Tammy's apartment. He had intended to go home and shower before work, but the announcement Tammy made knocked that idea on its head.

'Jake?' Jenny persisted.

Jake's jaw tightened. Why hadn't his assistant followed true to form and strolled into work late armed with coffee and excuses? 'I could ask you the same question,' he said sharply.

'I didn't want to get fired,' she replied demurely.

'Didn't know it was that easy to get rid of you,' he muttered. Although, damn it all, he couldn't do without her. She might seldom be on time, might interfere with his life, but she knew to the second where he should be and when.

Besides which, she was his friend. He sighed. Thank God for friends like Jenny. Thank God she never took offense.

'Want some coffee?' she asked.

'Black,' he answered gratefully.

She cast him another glance as she passed his desk, her sharp gaze roving from his crumpled clothes to his chin. A chin he hadn't had time to shave.

Jake looked away. He couldn't allow Jenny to see his worry. If she did, her questions would never end. He fixed his gaze instead on the wall opposite, and prayed the new paint would do as Jenny promised. Peace and serenity, she had said, would be his for the asking with moss-green walls.

It was too soon for serenity to be forthcoming. That wouldn't happen until he knew things were all right with Tammy and with the baby if there should be one. Jenny returned and handed him his coffee along with a disapproving glance.

'I thought you intended on an early night,' she said. 'You look as though you've spent the last ten hours on a bus.'

Jake didn't answer, concentrated instead on breathing in the Java, willing the coffee's scent to clear the confusion from his brain. He gulped down a mouthful, not caring that the hot liquid burned his throat.

Jenny sat in the chair on the other side of his desk and looked at him through narrowed eyes. 'Isn't that the same shirt you wore yesterday?' she accused.

'I have dozens of white shirts.' He placed his cup next to the phone.

'And that's the same tie.' Jenny's eyes darkened. Her pulled-back blonde hair escaped from its ribbon. 'It's the spare one you keep at work. You wore it yesterday to the meeting with Peterson Electronics. After,' she added triumphantly, 'you spilled jelly from your donut onto your blue one.'

Which he'd asked Jenny to wash, Jake realized, with a groan, to which she'd replied tartly that she was a personal assistant not a cleaner. Although once she'd made her position clear, she'd snatched the tie from around his neck and marched it into the coffee room muttering dire predictions of stains setting in if you didn't deal with them immediately.

He'd been glad of her help then. Didn't want it now.

'You missed your calling,' he said, from between clenched teeth. 'You should have been a detective.'

'Much more fun helping you. So,' she persisted, looking more cheerful now she'd reduced his evasions to rubble, 'what did you get up to last night?'

'I went out with Tony.'

'Tony! I haven't seen him since you moved your stuff over to his place. How's he doing?'

'Fine.' For a disorganized guy, Tony's life flowed without a ripple. No doubt *his* girlfriends never told him they were pregnant. Then, without warning, the face of the woman Tony had been talking to at the bar burst into Jake's brain with the clarity of crystal.

Dark hair, amazing eyes . . . there was something about her eyes. Despite the bar's flashing light and the expanse of space between them, Jake had seen the blue brilliance in the girl's eyes, had even recognized a familiarity.

As though he had met her somewhere before.

As though it was himself rather than Tony with whom she should be laughing. But by the time he'd maneuvered his way to where they sat, the woman had disappeared and Tammy had arrived.

The weight he'd been carrying since Tammy's announcement doubled. He couldn't think about Tony's woman, had to concentrate instead on getting through the time until Tammy called, until she told him for certain if she was carrying his child.

Jake pulled out the file he'd been

working on the day before, but couldn't seem to make out any of the words. The only letters he could see now were burned into his brain: B-A-B-Y, where they flashed on and off like a neon sign.

Jenny took the file from his hand. 'You promised to take me with you the next time you went out,' she reminded him.

'I promised nothing.'

'You said you'd introduce me to some of your friends.'

'I didn't promise. You begged.'

She lifted one brow. 'You said yes.'

'I did not. I wouldn't wish your badgering on any of my friends.'

'I don't badger,' she protested.

'Morning, noon and night, until you get your own way.'

'So long,' she replied, her lips tilting to a grin, 'as that's how it ends up.'

'Ruling my life,' he told her sternly, 'is not in your job description.'

'Neither is fetching your coffee, but I do some things for free.'

Jake turned away. Sparring with Jenny usually got his head into the thrust and parry an attorney's job required, but right now all he wanted was control of his life, not arguments with a woman who could read him like a book.

Jenny's smile disappeared. 'Are you all right?' she asked worriedly.

'I'm fine,' he replied.

'Because if you need an aspirin with that coffee — '

'Damn it, Jenny, I'm fine.'

'Is it the renovations making you crazy? How are they going?'

'Slowly.' Too slowly. And if Tony was seeing that woman in the bar, he didn't want to be around and have to watch them together. No matter how much he was enjoying reconnecting with his college roommate, he was used to his own space. Things would be much better when he could move back into his own place.

'Right,' Jenny went on. 'Shall I let Mr. Prescott know that you're in?'

'Prescott!' Jake straightened. 'What does he want?'

'To see you,' she replied. 'He said to let him know the minute you got here.'

'Don't tell him I'm here.' The thought of a conversation with the other senior partner of Prescott, Cummings and Mallory caused the pounding to increase in Jake's head.

'You should see him,' Jenny advised.

'I don't want to see anyone.' Jake leaned back into his plush leather chair and tried to relax. He normally didn't mind that Prescott relied on him, just as the old man had relied on Jake's father before he died, but this wasn't the moment for one of Prescott's rambling conversations. He had to instead wait for the phone to ring and hear Tammy say she wasn't pregnant with his child.

The possibility of becoming a father socked him in the gut anew. When the hell was Tammy going to phone?

Jenny eyed him suspiciously. 'There is something wrong. Tell me!'

11

Jake's fatigue deepened. It felt as though he hadn't slept at all last night. He didn't want to talk or go to court and argue cases. He wanted only to go home, drink coffee and read the paper, and pretend that he was still in charge of his life.

'You might as well tell me and get it over with,' Jenny prodded. 'It'll save us both a lot of time.'

It wasn't the baby from whom he wished to escape, for he'd always envisioned a future containing a child. But in his dreams he'd always loved the child's mother, with the sort of love his own parents had shared.

Not a short-term relationship based solely on sex.

Which was all that he and Tammy had wanted.

'A burden shared is a burden halved,' Jenny intoned.

'Not this time.' Jake glanced at his desk clock. Only eight forty-five. Tammy wouldn't even be at the doctor's yet. He had wanted to go with

12

her, but she had told him no. She would phone him, she had promised, and tell him what the doctor said.

'It's not about work,' Jenny mused aloud, 'or I'd know about it already. So it must have something to do with last night.'

'It's none of your business,' Jake said irritably.

'We're friends,' she reminded him quietly.

'Don't you have some work to do?'

'Nothing pressing.' She grinned. 'So where did you and Tony go?'

'Out,' he replied. 'I told you that.'

'Out where?' she asked.

'Fresco's bar.'

'Did you meet anyone?'

'Jenny,' he warned.

'Jake,' she replied.

'No one,' he lied.

She stretched across his desk and plucked a blonde hair off his jacket. 'No one?' she asked, her right brow lifting.

He sagged against his chair. 'All right,' he admitted. 'I met a woman.'

She held the hair up to the light. 'It seems you got to know her pretty well.'

Jenny couldn't have been more wrong. He and Tammy had only been dating a couple of months, and in that time they'd scarcely talked. Neither had been looking for anything permanent. They'd both simply enjoyed a laugh and a warm bed.

They weren't laughing now. When he'd gone home with her the night before it had been with the intention of breaking things off, but before he got the chance, she had told him of her condition.

He felt a sudden chill. What if she hadn't? The thought of a child he'd fathered being born without his knowledge made him feel ill.

'You went home with her, didn't you?' Jenny accused. She shook her head. 'When you left work last night, you promised you'd get some rest. You've been working twelve hours a day for weeks.'

'I'm fine,' he said sharply.

14

A frown line formed between her eyes. 'When you've been working really hard, you have to take care of yourself.'

'Speaking of work . . . ' He waved his hand in the direction of the door, and beyond the door to where her desk sat.

She stayed where she was. 'Work isn't everything.'

'I know that, Jenny. That's why I went out with Tony.'

'So what are you worried about?' Her expression softened. 'You've been an incredible friend to me and Sam, Jake. If you're in trouble, let me help.'

Jake wasn't sure if it was the mention of Jenny's twelve-year-old son that prompted his sudden desire to discuss the situation with her, or the fact she had experience in matters of impending parenthood. Only previously, Jenny had been the one pregnant, while his best friend Matt had been the baby's father.

'Try me,' she urged. 'You know I owe you big time.'

'You don't owe me a thing.'

'I don't know what I would have

15

done without you when I became pregnant,' she said softly.

He could still remember Matt telling him the news, telling him also that the baby wasn't his. 'You'd have been fine without me,' Jake told her gruffly.

'You stuck by me,' Jenny insisted, her eyes turning misty, 'when everyone else was running in the opposite direction.'

Not something he would let happen to Tammy.

'And,' Jenny went on, 'you got me this job.'

'You only like it because it gives you a chance to push me around.'

She laughed out loud. 'If only I could! You always do exactly what you want.'

'We don't always get what we want,' he replied grimly.

'Is that what's worrying you? You want something you can't have?'

'Not exactly.'

'Then what?' She frowned. 'Has this anything to do with the blonde woman?'

16

'Maybe.' He rolled his shoulders, tried unsuccessfully to ease his tension. 'Her name is Tammy. She says she's pregnant.'

Jenny's face turned pale.

'And she says the baby's mine.'

'What do you say?' Jenny asked.

'I've barely had time to think, let alone say anything.'

'You must have said something.'

'I asked her if she was sure.'

Jenny's brow scrunched up. 'Sure about what — that she's pregnant or that the baby is yours?'

'The first . . . the second . . . ' He lifted his shoulders. 'Maybe both.'

'And is she?'

'She's going to the doctor today, but she says she's as sure as she can be that she's pregnant. She also says it couldn't have been anyone else's but mine.'

'What did you say to that?'

'I told her if she's pregnant she can count on me.'

'Oh, Jake,' Jenny wailed.

'Yeah, well . . . ' He shrugged. 'You

know me and babies.'

'What about you and women?'

'What about me and women?'

'You're like cream to a cat with women. They come after you with their tongues hanging out.'

'I like them, too,' he admitted ruefully. Liked their shapes and their scent and the touch of their skin, liked their heat and their sounds and the warmth of their loving. Although lately he'd been wanting more than just the physical, wanted instead to know what was in their hearts and minds.

All of which took time. Unfortunately time for him was in short supply.

'You're handsome,' Jenny went on, regarding him thoughtfully.

He laughed. 'That's not what you usually say.'

' — and smart — '

'Without two brain cells to rub together — '

' — rich — '

'Not after this year's taxes!'

' — and charming when you want to

be. Some would say a good catch.'

He lifted one brow. 'You think Tammy's trying to catch me?'

'It's a possibility.'

'I thought you'd be on her side.'

'I'm *your* friend,' Jenny replied. 'Do you want my help or not?'

'Not.'

'You need me.'

'To do what?'

She leaned towards him across the table. 'To save you from your own good nature.'

'I'm not going into this blindly,' he said gently, 'but if Tammy is pregnant and I'm the father, I'm not running away.'

'I'm not suggesting you should.' Her expression grew grim. 'You're one of the good guys.'

'I'm glad you think so. It means a lot.'

'So you shouldn't have to serve a lifetime for something you haven't done. Did you use protection?' she suddenly asked.

'Of course.' He grimaced. 'But the condom broke.'

Jenny groaned.

As he had done when it happened, but Tammy had said forget it, then had kissed him so thoroughly he'd done just that.

'I do want kids,' he went on quietly. 'There's nothing I'd like better. It's just . . . whenever I imagined having them, it wasn't like this.'

'No one ever imagines this.'

'I thought I'd fall in love — '

'You've been too busy falling into bed.'

' — get married — '

'You like women too much to settle for just one.'

' — be committed — '

'You're married to your job.'

'I have been,' he admitted. 'But I don't want to be anymore. This sex with no strings isn't what I want. If Tammy isn't pregnant I intend to do things differently.'

'What do you mean?'

'I'd like to get to know a woman properly before we sleep together.'

Jenny looked at him dubiously. 'People always say that when they've been caught with their hand in the cookie jar.'

'I mean it,' he growled. 'If Tammy's pregnancy is a false alarm, I'm swearing off women. At least, I'm swearing off having sex with them.'

Jenny smiled. 'But for how long? You like women too much to give them up.'

'I intend to try.'

'Better set a time limit,' she suggested.

'What do you mean?'

'Sooner or later . . . and I predict sooner . . . your testosterone will get the better of you.'

'I'm not some teenager with no self-control!'

'It's not just you that has a say.'

He leaned back into his chair and tried to ignore her, tried to let his thoughts clarify in his mind. 'I'll woo a woman first,' he finally said, 'learn her

21

thoughts and desires before making love to her.'

Jenny shook her head. 'How long do you think that will take? One date, two, a week perhaps?'

'I don't care if it takes all summer.'

'You intend to swear off sex until the end of August?' Jenny's eyes filled with disbelief. 'There's no way you can make it that long.'

'Count on it,' he said firmly.

'I'll bet on it,' she said, her lips widening to a grin. 'Although I might have to take the summer off.'

'Why?' he asked.

'Without sex you're going to end up like a bear without honey. I don't want to be around for that.'

'Don't be ridiculous. It'll be easy.'

'Easy?' a voice demanded from the doorway of his office.

2

If she'd realized who it was before she had spoken, Melissa D'Angelo would have turned tail and run. As she'd done the night before when she spotted Jake Mallory in the bar.

But here in his office running away was impossible.

She only wished she'd had some sort of warning, for butterflies had taken flight in her belly. The ability to breathe should require no thought, but here she was, struggling for air.

'I knocked,' she said, scarcely able to get the words out. She'd been only sixteen when the same thing had occurred before, and that was the first time she had met Jake. Last night in the bar, despite the expanse of mate-seeking singles between them, the sentence she'd begun before setting eyes on Jake had trailed away to nothing, prompting her cousin Tony to comment that if four years at university had rendered her speechless, it was a great idea that she do four more.

'I know you,' Jake murmured, unfolding long legs to get to his feet. His dark eyes narrowed and on his unshaven chin, a shadow of beard showed blue.

'I don't think so,' she lied. With luck he wouldn't remember the day seven years before when, during a university term break, Tony had brought Jake Mallory to a D'Angelo family barbeque. The instant she'd laid eyes on her cousin's roommate, she had become a love-struck teenager. One who had followed Jake around doing embarrassing things in an effort to make him take notice of her.

The last news she had heard regarding him had been after Jake graduated and it was that he had been accepted into Harvard Law School. When he chose to do his Articles in New York city, she had never expected him to move back to Seattle.

24

Had never expected to end up in the same bar.

Mel stifled a sigh. If she hadn't been so busy with her final undergraduate exams, she might have seen Tony at least once since Christmas. And he might have mentioned his friend Jake in passing.

Then she wouldn't have been so shocked seeing Jake face to face, wouldn't want to flee as she did now. The woman opposite Jake rose from her seat. 'Can we help you?' she asked.

'The receptionist said to come through to this office.' What she hadn't been told was that the office was Jake's, the man who had set fire to her adolescent dreams.

'I'm Jake Mallory,' he said, holding out his hand.

Reluctantly Mel held out her hand also, battling an old desire to kiss him instead. Only the reserve instilled by her grandmother stopped that inclination, for an entire line of D'Angelo women would turn in their graves rather than kiss a stranger.

Jake's strong, warm palm engulfed her fingers. 'What can I do for you?' he asked.

Ridiculous . . . juvenile . . . to be rendered so giddy by the touch of a man, especially one who had obviously forgotten her.

Her friend Trish was right. She spent far too much time studying and not nearly enough time dating. She needed a man, a flesh and blood man, not fantasies left over from her teens.

A line formed between Jake Mallory's eyes. 'Are you all right?' he asked.

'Yes,' she murmured hastily then just as swiftly added, 'No.' She pulled away her hand and took a step backward, lifted her chin and forced all physical reactions from her mind. 'I want you to explain,' she said sternly, 'why you've treated my friend so badly.'

'What friend?' Jake demanded, his eyes suddenly growing dark, as black as the hair sweeping back from his face.

'Ms. Jessica Parker.'

Jake shook his head. 'I don't know any Jessica Parker.'

'Then your memory,' Mel said coolly, 'is obviously as faulty as your advice. Jessie consulted you last week.'

Jake turned to his assistant. 'Could you check the files, Jenny?'

'Right away.' The woman swept past Mel on her way to the door.

'Take a seat,' Jake offered, gesturing to the chair his assistant had vacated. He lowered himself back into his own leather chair.

Reluctantly Mel sat. She had never imagined Jake behind the massive oak of a lawyer's desk, but looking at him now, she saw that he suited it. He'd always had a commanding presence, and the desk seemed an extension of his power and strength. Hastily, she shifted her attention back to the task at hand. 'You can't have forgotten Jessie.'

'I think you've made a mistake.'

'You advised her to pay.'

'Pay whom?' Jake asked.

'Her lover,' Mel replied.

Jake's smiled. 'You'd better start at the beginning.'

Mel's cheeks grew hot. 'If you're going to treat this as a joke, then I won't waste my time.' She pushed herself into a standing position.

Jake Mallory stood also, and more rapidly than she'd have thought possible for such a big man, rounded the desk and took her arm.

Thank heavens she was wearing her turtle-necked cotton shirt, for the perspiration suddenly moistening her brow could be blamed on overdressing on an unusually hot day rather than her body's reaction to the chemistry of Jake.

He snatched his hand away. Had he too felt the heat?

'Sit down, Ms. . . . ?'

'Melissa.' Further words dried unspoken in her mouth. She couldn't decide what was more infuriating, the fact he didn't remember her or that he still had such an effect on her equilibrium. With an inelegant thump, she sat back into her chair.

'Tell me everything,' he demanded.

If she had a choice, she'd tell him nothing. But although Jessie was her employer, she was also her friend. Melissa cared for her, wanted to help her all she could. She cleared her throat. 'Miss Parker is being sued by the man she used to live with.'

'Live with?' Mallory repeated, jotting down something on a pad of yellow paper. 'She's not married then?'

'Jessie doesn't believe in marriage.' A fact which would have horrified Mel's grandmother if she were still alive, as it had the parish priest when Jessie espoused this view to him.

'Most women,' Jake murmured, not looking up as he wrote, 'find marriage to be a useful institution.'

'Not Jessie,' Mel replied. 'She says no paper is enough to keep a couple together, not if they want to be apart.' Jessie had said plenty more on the subject of sex, love and commitment,

29

but Mel had no intention of going into that with Jake.

He frowned and glanced up. 'What do you think?'

'This isn't about me.' She forced her gaze from his mouth, found it drawn instead by his sexy dark eyes.

'How long did they live together?'

'Eighteen months.' Mel straightened, but found her attention wandering to the dimple denting Jake's right cheek.

She tried to remember what she'd learned in first year Psychology, that animal magnetism was a normal reaction to a set of stimuli, not something that had to be acted upon. In fact, restraint was what kept people from behaving like lesser mammals.

Trish would disagree. Go for it, she'd have said if she was here.

Mel sucked in a breath, determined to do no such thing. 'About a month ago,' she went on, 'Jessie asked Tom to move out.' She shifted her attention to the paper on Jake's desk, tried not to let it wander next to the way his hair curled around his ears.

She realized anew how right Trish had been. She did need a man, needed to make love, if only to get rid of the feelings she'd been having lately, feelings that were distracting her from her work. She had to see for herself what all the fuss was about. At twenty-four years of age, almost twenty-five, it was long past time she had a lover.

Jake added a note to the pad before him. 'So Tom moved out of his house?' He glanced up. 'What's Tom's last name?'

'Preston, Tom Preston. But it's Jessie's house, not Tom's.'

'Ms. Parker's?' Frowning, Jake jotted a question mark next to a notation.

'Yes!' Mel exclaimed. 'And now he's suing her for support!'

'You must have your facts backwards.'

'What do you mean?'

'Surely it's Ms. Parker who is suing Mr. Preston for support?'

'Jessie was right,' Mel said stiffly. 'She told me not to come. She said there'd be no point.'

'Why would she think that?'

'She said all men stick together.'

'I stick with my client.' He gazed at Mel thoughtfully. 'Once I take one on that is.'

'Jessie said you advised her to pay, and that you also said Tom's entitled to half of everything she owns. That can't be right.'

'I never said — '

'She worked hard for her money,' Mel said, interrupting. 'She shouldn't have to share it with a no-good lay-about.'

'Is that what Mr. Preston is?'

'Yes.' Mel bit her lip. 'At least, that's what Jessie says.'

Jake frowned. 'Where is Ms. Parker? Why isn't she here to tell me the facts herself?'

'She says she's already talked to you. She doesn't want to pay twice for going over the same details.'

'I've never met Ms. Parker,' he repeated patiently.

'Are you calling Jessie a liar?'

'No . . . just mistaken.'

'There's no mistake.' But unease pricked the hair on the nape of Mel's neck. Jessie's usual sharp wit had been absent at times lately, leaving her uncertain of details, facts and dates. She had, however, been adamant about her visit to Mallory's law office, had told Mel everything that had been discussed.

'Where does Ms. Parker work?' Jake's pen was poised above his note pad.

'Work!' Mel exclaimed. 'She's eighty-two years old!'

'Eighty-two?' Jake's eyes widened. 'Now I'm sure I haven't met her.' He shot Mel a rueful smile. 'An octogenarian keeping a lover would stand out in any crowd. How old is he, by the way?'

'A bit younger than Jessie.' Mel couldn't help smiling also. 'She likes younger men.'

'How much younger?'

'He's seventy-nine.'

'Not exactly a toy boy.'

'Not exactly.' Mel chuckled. 'Tom's bald, except for his comb-over, and he's got a pot belly. He's a bit bowlegged, but not enough to make it difficult to walk.'

'A sex God?' Jake murmured, his smile expanding to a grin.

'Something like that.' When Jake smiled like that, warmth flowed through her. If she was going to keep this conversation business-like, he had to stop smiling.

'Ah, Jenny,' he said suddenly, looking over Mel's shoulder.

Mel glanced around. She hadn't heard Jake's assistant enter.

Jenny drew past Mel's chair and dropped a file on Jake's desk. 'I think this is what you're looking for.'

Jake opened the folder and swiftly scanned a page. 'This explains it,' he said, at last, glancing up at Mel. 'It was James Mallory who saw your Ms. Parker.'

34

Mel frowned. 'Who's James Mallory?'

'My uncle,' Jake replied.

The telephone on Jake's desk suddenly rang, and Jake jumped as though a starter pistol had gone off.

'Shall I get that?' Jenny asked.

'No,' Jake said sharply, but rather than answering the phone, he stared at it as though it were a snake ready to strike. 'Excuse me,' he said to Mel. 'I've been expecting a call.' He reached for the receiver now, his jaw line tightening, and he held the phone so hard, his knuckles turned white. 'Did you do as we discussed?' he asked, in a low voice, then after listening for an instant, asked, 'What did the doctor say?' He half turned away, his shoulders straining against the fabric of his jacket.

He should take it off, Mel thought. Then, her cheeks warming, she tried to shift her attention elsewhere. But, as the lines in a picture lead the eye to the main subject, all paths in this room seemed to travel back to Jake.

Which only went to show how sex-crazed she had become. She couldn't go around obsessing about a man, even one with whom she'd once imagined herself in love. If she wanted him, she should ask him out. Times had changed Trish had told her, making it acceptable now for a woman to make the first move. But — Mel shivered — that didn't help if the woman was shy.

'Right,' Jake finally said, shifting the phone to his other hand. Then, 'Right,' he said again, with a shrug of his shoulders.

Mel couldn't tell whether the movement was to shake off a burden or in silent response to his correspondent's question, but she suddenly had the urge to take hold of his hand, to hug him and tell him everything would be all right.

'I'll call you later.' Then slowly, carefully, he hung up the receiver.

'Was it . . . ?' Jenny asked.

'Yes,' he answered quickly.

36

'Is she . . . ?'

'Apparently not.'

'Then you're not . . . ?'

'No.'

A broad smile appeared on Jenny's lips. 'Would you like a coffee,' she asked, turning to Mel, 'or perhaps some tea?'

'No, thank you.' Mel stood. 'I'll go now. If Mr. Mallory's not the lawyer Jessie saw last week, there's no point in my taking up any more of his time.' If she left immediately she might be able to get out before Jake realized who she was, and remember her embarrassing antics of seven years before.

'Stay,' Jake ordered, rising also to his feet. 'My uncle's away for the next few weeks. I've promised to take over some of his cases while he's gone. I need a brief word with Jenny, then I'd like to discuss Ms. Parker's situation with you further.'

He should have let her go. Melissa D'Angelo's scent engulfed Jake again as it had the moment she arrived, flowery, yet subtle, more tangy than sweet. And he still had the feeling he'd met her before, not simply seen her in the bar the previous night. But if that had been the case he would never have forgotten her. A woman like her, with those eyes . . . those lips.

Her smile lit the room as it had lit her corner of the bar the night before, had lit something inside him as well. He stood, and followed Jenny towards the door. 'I'll just be a moment,' he told Mel again.

The minute the door closed behind them, Jenny threw her arms around Jake's neck. 'I'm so glad!' she exclaimed. 'Everything's all right.'

'Yes,' he said, but he didn't feel as happy as he had expected. He waited for relief to overtake him, but all that came was a dull ache in his chest.

'What about Tammy?' Jenny asked. 'How's she feeling?'

'Relieved,' he replied. The pain spread to his temples, then pounded clear through his head. When he'd heard the relief in Tammy's voice, he hadn't expected that disappointment would flood his own heart.

'That's all right then,' Jenny said. 'Although,' she added. 'Now you've got another problem.'

'What sort of problem?'

'Your promise.' Jenny smiled. 'Sex,' she added clearly. 'No more sex for the entire summer.'

'No problem,' Jake said. He could do without sex, could especially do without this feeling of loss.

'We should make it interesting,' Jenny went on.

He eyed her warily. 'What do you mean?'

'You double my summer's salary if you fail to keep your vow? And,' she added, 'you promise to introduce me to an eligible man?'

'What do I get when I win the bet?'

Jenny chuckled. 'The satisfaction of knowing you have self-control.'

'I know that already.'

'Prove it,' she challenged.

Jake stood perfectly still, imagining life without the warmth of a woman.

Jenny's eyes narrowed. 'I hope you're not planning on backing out?'

'Of course not,' he growled.

'Because a bet's a bet.'

'Nothing to it.' He turned on his heel and re-entered his office. Tony's woman was now standing next to his window, and for some unknown reason had taken off her sweater.

Revealing beneath a spaghetti-strapped top.

Outside in the corridor, he'd thought the bet would be easy. Suddenly, he realized that it wasn't. The top was bright red and startlingly sexy, especially topping as it did her short swinging skirt, which in return revealed long shapely legs. A sight he was normally free to appreciate.

She turned to face him and her hair lifted in a flowing wave. Like a woman from a television shampoo commercial . . . unnatural . . . unreal . . . yet totally enticing.

Sunlight poured through the window, illuminating her face. Most women preferred candlelight to the full force of the morning sun, but Melissa's skin needed no hiding, and the only lines on her face had been put there by laughter.

He could look at her all day. He shouldn't look at her at all.

'I've got to go,' she said softly.

'We're not done,' he replied.

Perspiration suddenly beaded her forehead.

He ran a finger beneath his collar. 'It's hot in here.' He wished it was winter. In winter Seattle would be drowning in icy rain, and if it was clear, would be frosty cold.

'Yes,' Miss D'Angelo agreed. She lifted her hair with hands that seemed unsteady, and twisted its bulk into a knot. Immediately, it fell out into a curtain around her shoulders.

'Summer's coming,' she added, her tongue darting out to moisten her lips.

June, July, August.

Three whole months.

A long time to give up the fairer sex. Tony's woman took a step forward, seemed to want to pass by. Instead, as she moved, her arm tangled with his.

'Sorry,' she murmured, her cheeks turning pink. Her eyes, now closer, widened and grew dark.

'My fault,' he replied, intending to step aside. But he took her hand instead. He tried not to pull her closer, but staring into her eyes, he felt as though he held a drink he couldn't down. 'You'd better go,' he said softly.

Her eyes glazed, grew confused. 'Why don't you — ?' She stopped.

'Don't I what?' he demanded.

'Kiss me?' she replied, lifting her chin. 'I can feel that you want to.'

3

'He kissed you?' Trish asked, her green eyes widening.

'No,' Mel replied. She glanced around the crowded coffee café and prayed the two smartly dressed women at the next table hadn't heard the embarrassing details of her lack of love life. To her relief they seemed too engrossed in their own gossip to be interested in hearing anything of hers.

'What then?' Trish demanded in a too-loud voice.

Her friend's red hair was as explosive as her voice. It burst from the purple elastic binding it, whirling out in all directions like sun-kissed cotton candy.

Mel took a sip of her hot chocolate, and hoped the delay in answering would cool her burning cheeks. Finally, she put her hot chocolate down. 'He leaned forward,' she said, 'as though he was going to kiss me.'

'And then?'

'He leaned away.'

'Hmm,' Trish said thoughtfully. 'Why, do you think?'

A question Mel had asked herself at least a dozen times, but every answer she came up with was less than flattering. 'Kissing people in law offices,' she finally said, 'is really not appropriate.'

'There's nothing sacred about a law office.' Her friend shot her a swift grin. 'I made love once in an elevator of a building that held nothing but law offices.'

'Trish!' Mel exclaimed.

'Don't look so horrified.' Her friend chuckled. 'I was going out with Dave then. You remember him. Short, sticky-out ears, and too-big feet. But,' she sighed, 'I thought he was cute.'

'But in an elevator!' Mel said.

'The building was new. None of the offices were occupied yet. There was no one there to see us.' Trish's cheeks turned a rosy hue. 'It was exciting. You should try it.'

Mel shuddered. 'I wouldn't be able to concentrate. I'd be too terrified someone would come.'

'You don't concentrate on sex. You just let it flow. And the fear of discovery is half the fun.'

'Not for me,' Mel said emphatically. When she made love, especially for the first time, it would be somewhere private, somewhere she and her lover could block out the world.

Trish moved the sugar dish to one side then leaned forward across the table. 'So tell me what he's like, this lawyer friend of yours?'

'He's not my friend.' She couldn't tell Trish she'd met Jake years before, for her friend would spin some fantasy of destiny and fate.

'He's something,' Trish teased. 'Possible lover, perhaps?'

'Fantasy lover, maybe.' Heat climbed Mel's neck. 'I won't be seeing him again.'

'Why not?' Trish demanded. 'Phone him up. Ask him out.'

'I couldn't.'

'You could. He'd jump at the chance.'

Mel shook her head. 'I doubt he's the sort of guy who's short of dates. He probably has women lined up around the block.'

'Why? What does he look like?'

'Tall,' Mel replied, then frowned at the dreamy tone infiltrating her voice. 'Dark,' she hurried on. 'Handsome,' she added.

'He sounds perfect,' Trish said.

'I was seeing him on business,' Mel replied firmly.

'Nothing wrong with combining pleasure with business.'

Mel noted with unease the excited look in Trish's eyes, a look that in the past had guaranteed Mel embarrassment. 'I don't think so,' she said.

'Do you want to have fun, or not?' Trish pulled out her cell phone.

'Not,' Mel said decisively.

'Nonsense.' Trish thrust the phone towards her.

Mel held the phone with the tips of her fingers. 'What do you expect me to do with this?'

'Phone him,' Trish replied.

'I don't know his number.'

'Dial information.'

Mel handed the phone back. 'I am not going to phone him. I'll probably never see him again.' She was certainly not going back to his office. She'd tell Jessie to find someone else to act as her legal go-between. At sixteen, it was excusable to make an idiot of oneself. At almost twenty-five, it certainly was not.

'If you want this man, you've got to go after him,' Trish insisted.

'What happened to the concept of the male chasing the female?'

Her friend grinned. 'That's never been the natural order of things. Women orchestrate and men do as they're told.'

'I can't see Jake Mallory following

anyone's command.'

'He will if you work it right. You'll have him begging out of your hand.'

'Stay, sit, beg?' Mel said dubiously.

'You just have to give him the right reward.'

Mel frowned.

'Don't look so worried. Making a man do what you want is easy.'

'Maybe for you,' Mel muttered. 'You've had experience.'

'You've had some, too.'

'Not so as you'd notice.'

'What about that guy from your chemistry class last year?'

'I didn't actually go out with him.'

'You had coffee.'

Mel wrinkled her nose. 'All we did was discuss our lab notes.'

'You study too much.'

'I have to,' Mel said.

'Not anymore,' Trish said sternly. 'The time for studying so hard is over. You've now made it into the hallowed halls of medical school. It's time you had a little fun.'

'Med school is when the real work begins.'

'Not until September. You've got the whole summer to date, drink and be merry.'

'I'm not sure I know how.' Mel stared thoughtfully down into her hot chocolate then took another sip.

'For starters,' Trish said, taking hold of Mel's cup and pulling it away, 'you've got to develop a taste for cappuccino. Hot chocolate is not sexy.'

'I didn't know it had to be.'

'Coffee bars are great places for women to meet men, but the women guys are looking for are sophisticated and chic.'

'Cappuccino is chic?' Had Trish finally lost her mind?

'Totally,' her friend replied. 'It's Italian.'

'I'm Italian.'

'A generation removed. Not the same thing at all.' Trish turned an assessing gaze on her. 'And we're talking about coffee, not women. You never see glamorous women with hot chocolate mustaches.'

Mel swiped her upper lip, was relieved to find it dry.

'Glamorous women . . . sexy women, either drink wine or expensive coffee.'

A swift glance at the table next to them verified Trish's words. Mel frowned and turned her attention back to her friend. 'I don't like cappuccino,' she insisted, 'and I'm not going to drink it just to please some guy.'

'Even Jake Mallory?'

'No.'

'Liar,' Trish accused. But with a sigh, she handed back Mel's hot chocolate. 'I'll have to take you in hand. Introduce you to some men.'

Mel grinned. 'You make it sound like the thirteenth labor of Hercules.'

'It might be,' Trish said solemnly. 'You don't go out much — '

'I'm out now!'

'You live in the suburbs — '

'I'm not that far out of town.'

'No guy is going to spend forty-five

minutes driving to the burbs, then back into town for dinner, then back again to your house to drop you off home.' Trish slumped against the metal table. 'I'm exhausted just thinking about it, and I'm your friend!'

'I suppose it is a little far.'

'So why are you still living at home?'

'You know why!' Mel exclaimed. 'Since Nona died — '

'Your grandmother died two years ago!' Trish exclaimed.

Mel caught her lip between her teeth, felt again the familiar pain that had followed Nona's death. 'There's my dad — '

'Your dad won't be lonely if you move out now,' Trish protested.

Mel frowned. Her father needed her. He had no one else. 'You know what Pop's like,' she went on. 'He needs to know I'm safe.' Wrapping their women in cotton wool was the habit of all D'Angelo men. Her uncle Paulo was the same, as was her cousin Tony. 'Pop thinks,' Mel explained, 'that even the university is a dangerous place.'

'Full of men on the prowl,' Trish said, with a chuckle, 'ready to take advantage of his little girl?'

'Something like that. And now that I've been accepted to medical school . . . '

'Surely your father's proud of that?'

'I'm not sure. It makes him nervous. He'd prefer it if I was in what he considers a female profession, not sitting in some science lab surrounded by men. He complains that he never knows what to say to Mrs. Nunzio.'

'Who on earth is Mrs. Nunzio?'

'Our neighbor down the street. She's always asking him when I'm going to get married.' Mel blew out some air. 'It's almost funny. Pop would love to see me safely married, but he doesn't want to admit that for that to happen, I would have to meet and fall in love with a man.'

'Most fathers feel like that.'

'Your father doesn't. And most fathers have wives to keep their worries in check.' Her mother had died when Mel was only six. Nona had lived with them since then.

'Which is why, girlfriend, you have got to move out! What your pop doesn't know won't worry him the slightest.' Trish's eyes lit up. 'You could move in with me!' She leaned forward excitedly. 'My apartment's not that big, but I've got that little room I've been using as a study.'

'Trish, I don't think — '

'That could be your room. I could move my computer into my bedroom, and clean out that extra dresser.'

'Trish, stop!' Mel ordered.

'Stop what?'

'Stop planning something that can never happen. I can't afford to move out.'

Trish gazed at her sternly. 'You can't afford not to.'

'What do you mean?'

'If you stay home much longer, you'll never have a life.'

'I have a life,' Mel asserted.

'If you've never had sex,' Trish pronounced solemnly, 'you don't have a life.'

'Plenty of people have never had sex.'

Trish gazed at her pityingly.

'All right,' Mel conceded. 'Maybe not plenty. But enough.'

'Do you really want to be one of them?'

'No.' Mel bit her lip. She was sick of being the only twenty-four-year-old virgin she knew. Up until now she'd been too busy studying to concern herself with men, had been afraid that if she put time and energy into a relationship, she might fail to attain her dream of becoming a doctor. But she couldn't be a doctor if she hadn't experienced sex.

Sex was a normal physiological function, necessary to the overall health of a human. She didn't want to become unhealthy. She especially didn't want to be unknowledgeable. And if she didn't make an effort to experience sex soon, she might lose her nerve.

'Move in with me,' Trish insisted.

'You can guarantee me sex?'

'Maybe not guarantee, but I'm willing to die trying.' Trish reached for Mel's hand. 'Tell your father,' she urged. 'It can't hurt to talk about it.'

★   ★   ★

'Set the table, Princess,' Mel's father instructed as he poured thick tomato sauce over the spaghetti he'd just boiled. The pungent scent of herbs and garlic filled the air.

Mel laid a cloth of the palest yellow over the oak table then set out the plates her grandmother had left her. Her fingers warmed at the familiar touch of the butter-yellow china that she mixed with her mother's set of Mediterranean blue, creating a table-top illusion of sun and sky.

She would wait until after dinner before she brought up the subject of moving out, until her father had pushed aside his plate and taken a final sip of the Chianti Uncle Paulo had brought home from Naples. Once Pops was relaxed, she'd find a way to slip her plans into the conversation.

She could only pray that the actual doing would be easier than the planning, and that it wouldn't feel as though she was plunging a knife into her father's back. 'Set an extra place,' her father directed, carrying the steaming food to the kitchen table. 'Tony said he might drop by.'

'Tony!' Mel exclaimed. 'Why's Tony coming?'

'Relatives don't need a reason to visit.'

'But I just saw him!'

Her father turned and looked at her. 'You did?'

'Yes.' Mel's heart sunk. She hadn't seen Tony for months and now she'd be seeing him twice in two days. If her cousin was coming, she'd have to tell her father she was moving before he got there.

With a few swift movements, she

tossed the romaine lettuce she'd prepared for the Caesar salad, cut focaccia bread into wedges and carried it all to the table. Then slowly, reluctantly, she dropped into her chair opposite her father.

Who turned to Mel and smiled.

Feeling like Judas, Mel smiled back.

Her father disposed of grace in his usual fashion, simply nodded to the picture of Jesus her grandmother had hung over the kitchen door and made the sign of the cross on his chest. If her grandmother had been alive, there'd have been more time for Mel to collect her thoughts, for her grandmother had always engaged in long discussions with the Lord.

Mel sucked in a deep breath. 'Pops,' she began.

'Mmm,' he replied, dipping a wedge of focaccia into a saucer of olive oil and balsamic vinegar.

'It's time I moved out,' she said baldly.

The bread in her father's hand

stopped halfway to his mouth. The oil and vinegar soaking it dripped to the table, creating a speck of black on the yellow cloth that proceeded to grow like an eclipse of the sun. Mel stared at it and thought, to those who didn't know better, an eclipse was a time of change and fear.

She wasn't afraid, she suddenly realized, at least not of moving out. The only thing she feared was worrying her father, and worry, even as she spoke, was etching itself onto his face.

Her father laid his bread on the edge of his plate and picked up his fork instead. He stabbed it into the spaghetti and began a twirling motion, not looking at Mel, not looking at his food either. He stared past her to the window overlooking their back garden. 'It's going to be a hot summer,' he finally said. 'It's a good thing we put in those extra tomato plants this year. The tomato sauce your grandmother canned is just about finished.'

All further words died in Mel's

throat. She had helped can those tomatoes the year her grandmother died. When they were done, they had stood side by side, arms around each other's waists, gazing with satisfaction at the rows of gleaming jars filled to the brim with spicy spaghetti sauce. Her father probably thought Mel would do the canning herself this year, would follow her grandmother's recipe and preserve the family tradition.

Which wouldn't be easy if she lived thirty miles away.

'You want to move out?' her father suddenly said, putting down his fork and giving her his full attention.

'Not for good, Pops,' she replied. 'Just for the summer. Trish asked me to move in with her for a few months.'

'She lives in the city.' Her father grimaced. 'Seattle's hot in the summer.'

'It's hot here too.'

'Not like in an apartment. There'll be no garden, no air.'

Maybe not, Mel thought, but there would be men.

'You'll be surrounded by strangers.' Her father uttered the word as though it was inconceivable for his daughter to choose strangers over neighbors she'd known her entire life.

'They won't be strangers for long,' Mel protested. 'Besides, Trish knows most of the people in her building.' Mel could only pray that if she did move in, her father would never meet the man in apartment twelve, who believed clothes to be restrictive and often went out into the hallway in the nude to dispose of his garbage down the chute.

Trish said no one minded, for her building housed mainly twenty-somethings, who regarded the man as a harmless sixties throwback, whose lava lamps and sitar music conjured up a more laid-back era.

Her father frowned. 'There would be no one at Trish's to take care of you, Princess.'

'I don't need taking care of. Besides,' she went on firmly, 'Trish and I will watch out for each other.'

'Trish!' Her father's frown deepened. 'Trish can't take care of herself, let alone you.'

'I'm a grown woman, Pops.'

'You're not even twenty-five.'

'Most women leave home when they're still in their teens.'

'None of the women in our family leave home until they marry.'

'I'm not getting married any time soon.' Marriage was a topic she didn't want to discuss. The last time Pops had brought it up, he had offered to enlist Mrs. Nunzio's services to introduce Mel to suitable young men.

'You can't move out,' her father decreed. 'You can't afford rent and medical school too.'

Mel stifled a gasp. Until this moment, her father had refused to even discuss medical school, probably hoping some miracle would occur and that instead of going to school, she'd get married instead.

'It'll only be for the summer,' she repeated. 'Trish won't charge me much.

I'll move home in September when I start school.'

'Home from where?' a deep voice suddenly asked.

Tony! Mel turned to find her cousin striding through the kitchen doorway. He tapped her shoulder in greeting, then edging past her, dropped onto the chair next to the window. Although he had asked the question, he didn't wait for an answer, but proceeded to dish pasta onto his plate.

'Well?' he finally said, after he'd swallowed his first mouthful. 'Where are you going?'

'Trish has asked me to move in with her,' Mel replied. 'And I've told her I will.'

'Trish!' Tony scowled. 'You don't want to live with her.'

'Why not?' Mel asked coolly.

'You won't like it,' he replied, calmly helping himself to bread and salad. 'Trish is pretty wild.'

'Wild!' Mel glared at him. 'She's got a job, friends . . . she's got a life.'

'I saw her at the Lava Lounge Monday night.' Tony stopped talking for a moment to chew another mouthful. 'With three guys and no other women.'

'Great odds,' Mel said, crossing her arms.

Her cousin reached for the Chianti and poured himself a glass. 'If you think I'm going to trust three guys with my cousin — '

'It's got nothing to do with you!'

'That's not what Nona said.'

Mel glowered at her steadily chewing cousin.

'Nona said,' he went on, 'that I was to watch out for you.'

'That was right after you hit me on the head with your baseball,' Mel replied furiously, 'and in case you've forgotten, I was eight years old at the time. Besides,' she went on, 'Trish works for an ad agency. She went out Monday night with the guys from the graphics department to celebrate the new campaign they've just launched.

Those men were co-workers, not dates. And — ' She took a deep breath. ' — there's nothing wrong with meeting men.'

Her father's face grew grimmer. 'I don't like it, Melissa.' He said her full name the way he always did, the vowels rolling off his tongue roundly then elongating at the end like a perfect musical note.

'It's time,' Mel said firmly. 'I was thinking of going to Trish's place tonight.'

'Tonight!' her father exclaimed.

'I want to check it out, get an idea of what I need to bring.'

'You can't go tonight,' her father said. 'We haven't talked about this properly.'

Mel cast her cousin a pleading look.

Tony scowled then gave her an almost imperceptible nod. 'Why doesn't she come back . . . ' The rest of his words were lost in a mouthful of romaine lettuce.

'Come back?' Mel asked sharply.

Tony swallowed his bite of salad. 'To

my place,' he finished. 'Just for tonight of course. Then I'll go with you to Trish's apartment in the morning.' He glanced at Mel's father. 'I'll check it out, Uncle Vince. I'll make sure she'll be safe.'

'I don't know,' Mel's father said. Frown lines cut a swath on his forehead. 'I better call Paulo. Mel can stay with him and Lilly.'

Melissa groaned. 'I don't need the whole family to be involved in my business.'

'It'll be all right,' Tony said firmly. 'I'll make sure her friend's place is suitable before she moves in.'

'Do you have room for her, Tony?'

'Both of my roommates are gone for the summer. I've sublet Pete's room to a friend who's redecorating his condo, but John's playing sax on one of the cruise ships, so his room is free.' He glanced at Mel with upraised brows. 'Come if you want to.'

Mel leaped to her feet and flung her arms around Tony's neck. 'Thank you,' she whispered into his ear.

'You owe me,' he whispered back.

* * *

Mel shifted Tony's briefcase from the front passenger seat of his Volkswagen van and settled there herself.

'Anything,' she said.

'Anything what?' Her cousin cursed under his breath at the grinding noise the engine made when he turned the key in the ignition.

'You said I owed you,' she replied. 'I'm willing to pay.'

'Just don't clean.' Tony shot her a grin as the van roared to a start. 'I've seen the results of that.'

'I'm not nine anymore,' Mel replied huffily.

'Maybe not.' His grin widened. 'But you're still not neat.'

'I'll have you know being a professional cleaner is part of my responsibilities at the moment.'

'God help those old folks,' Tony said.

'I haven't had any complaints.'

'Then their eyesight's probably bad.' Her cousin twisted the steering wheel and pulled out onto the road. 'Tell you what,' he added. 'Come over to my place one night when I have a date and cook up one of Nona's specialties. Then we'll call it even.'

'Done!' Mel agreed. They had both loved their grandmother's cooking, and cooking, at least, was something Mel did well. Her grandmother had taught her that food was not just fuel to keep the body going, but something to be shared with those you loved.

The image of Jake Mallory suddenly filled her mind. Mel shook her head. She'd have to keep in check this tendency to fantasize, would have to find a real man to cook for and seduce.

She'd earned her spot in medical school by organization and hard work. She'd apply those same skills to getting a man. Someone sexy, someone fun, someone definitely not interested in commitment.

Shouldn't be too difficult. From everything she'd ever read or heard, most men were happy to have sex without strings.

'I'll be keeping an eye on you, of course,' her cousin added.

Mel glanced at him swiftly, had almost forgotten he was there.

'Just following Nona's orders,' Tony said with an air of righteousness.

'Don't even think you're going to tell me what to do.'

He was no longer even looking at her. His attention was focused on merging onto the freeway. 'I'm watching out for you whether you like it or not.' Tony stepped hard on the gas and swerved over to the fast lane. 'Better get used to it.'

Mel pressed her lips tight. Tony could make all the pronouncements he wished, but no one was going to stop her from doing what she wanted. Despite all odds, she had been accepted into medical school. Finding one lusty man shouldn't prove anywhere near as difficult.

4

Mel breathed in the musky scent of male cologne and stretched her limbs beneath the silk sheets. If she could keep her eyes closed, she wouldn't have to wake up, wouldn't have to relinquish the hot lips on her skin.

Jake Mallory's lips.

His body was there, too, wrapped around hers, all hard lines and heat; wanting, persuading, cajoling her with his passion. Making her need in a way beyond thought, beyond conscious decision and life-changing choices. With a moan, her eyes opened. Slowly, confusedly, she stared around the room. The dream had seemed so real, but here the dream ended, in this room of her brother's friend, surrounded by male things.

Jake's presence, too, took a long moment to dissipate, as did the sensations that had rocked her to her core. She breathed deep, closed her mind, tried to un-touch what he had touched, but the memories lingered like headiness after wine.

She sat up, breathed again, forced away the desire. She didn't want lips formed by imagination, or a dream-world induced by wine before bed. She wanted lips that were real, better than any dream, but knew of no other way to connect with Jake Mallory.

She swung her feet to the floor, feeling as though she'd slept the afternoon away. She was due at Jessie's by ten, didn't want to be late. A swift glance at the clock on the bedside table scattered the panic beginning to swell. Only eight o'clock. She still had two hours. Into which time she could fit a visit to Trish's apartment.

A visit she wished to make without Tony's company. He'd told her the night before he'd be out when she got up as he had a few errands to do first thing. Which suited her just fine. She didn't need his seal of approval on Trish's place, didn't want him accompanying her as though she were a child.

When they were children, her grandmother could quell Tony with just a look, but at the same time had let Mel know that her cousin was simply doing what all male D'Angelos did, laying down the law and expecting to be obeyed. She hadn't obeyed then and didn't intend to start now, despite old promises Tony had made Nona.

She found her negligee in a heap on the floor, where she'd tossed it in the night during her dream-filled sleep. Sleeping naked had made her feel different already, as though the move into town had transformed her into a woman.

A woman capable of seducing a man.

Unfortunately not a woman with the body like that of the picture staring back at her from the wall. Tony's absent roommate had a classical taste in art, for the Degas print of a naked woman stepping into a wooden bath was a

study of curves and sensuous feminin-
ity.

Maybe once she made love, she'd be
sensuous too.

Throwing on her negligee, she
opened the bedroom door and moved
along the hall toward the bathroom.
She finished work at four today.
She'd ask Trish to meet her then for a
drink, and elicit her help in finding a
man.

She glanced in through Tony's open
bedroom door and scowled at the
evidence of her cousin's tidiness. Made
bed, dusted furniture, shoes all in a row
— they even had their heels against the
wall. It was amazing that a man who
chose to act for a living could have the
habits of a house-proud wife, while she,
a future doctor, whose life should be
filled with order, found it impossible to
put things away.

Another thing she'd have to change.
She'd make an effort to be neater, more
mature. It couldn't be that difficult if
Tony could manage it.

With a sigh, she grabbed the bathroom door knob and with a swift twist swung the door inward, landing her right into the naked chest of a man.

A chest so close all she could see was black hair whirling in soft patterns against tanned flesh. She could feel the hammer hardness of muscles against her cheek.

She thrust out her hand, intending to push the man away. Instead, strong fingers clasped her wrist in a grip of iron.

'Melissa,' a voice growled.

The voice from her dreams.

Jake Mallory's voice. And also his body.

She glanced down and saw what only intuition had told her, that Jake's muscular body was completely naked.

In the Biology classes she'd taken in University, she'd seen plenty of detailed diagrams of the human form, but nothing that prepared her for the detail she now saw; the thickness, the hardness, the symphony of strength.

Her breath disappeared. She tried to look away.

'Melissa,' Jake said again.

'Jake,' she whispered, breathing out his name.

Slowly, deliberately, scarcely appearing to move, he reached out his hand and took hold of a towel. When he wrapped it around his waist, she at last looked up.

'If I'd known you were here,' she said, her voice shaky, 'I would never have come in.' Not the sort of statement Trish would have made, but Mel hadn't expected to man-hunt in her own shower.

She wanted Jake more than she'd ever wanted anything, but at the same time, was terrified of her need.

His fingers tightened around her wrist. Her belly tightened in response. A single contraction, more pleasure than pain.

His gaze fixed on hers, with eyes so intense they penetrated clear through her. She lowered her gaze again and instantly regretted it, for his lips were the lips she'd dreamed of the night before.

The feelings coursing through her were what she had sought but not here, not now, not without preparation. Sex suddenly seemed a bigger deal in real life than it had in her made-up fantasy world, more important, more frightening, more ultimately final.

Which was why, in the first place, she'd decided to seek a sexual partner. So that the act wouldn't loom, growing ever larger in her mind, wouldn't overtake the energies she needed for her studies.

'What are *you* doing here?' she demanded. Perhaps conversation would somehow dissipate their attraction, would make her stop wanting his skin next to hers.

'I could ask you the same thing.'

'Tony invited me.' Desperately, she searched for the strength to step away, but despite the lava-hot blood in her veins, it appeared she was currently frozen to the floor.

'Tony!' He stiffened. 'So it *was* you I saw in the bar the other night.'

'I don't know,' she lied.

One black brow lifted.

He didn't believe her.

Why had she lied?

How could she not?

'It was two nights ago.' A line formed between his eyes.

She shrugged, tried to pretend she neither saw nor cared, but she still remembered the exact moment she had spotted Jake. She swallowed hard. 'You haven't answered my question. What are you doing here?'

'I live here,' he replied.

A bead of water rolled down from his hair and dropped to his shoulder, where it glistened for a moment before rolling to his chest. Mel noted with amazement that her hand was still splayed across him, and that if she moved fast she could catch the drip.

If Trish were here, she'd have licked the water away, the caress of her tongue turning into a kiss. From there things would lead into an embrace until, before they knew it, they'd be making love.

Sounded easy in theory.

Much harder in real life.

She wasn't Trish and she couldn't suddenly discard her inhibitions, especially with the man who for so long had filled her dreams.

'So?' Jake asked again.

'Tony's roommate's on a cruise ship,' she finally babbled out, clinging to the few facts Tony had imparted.

'Pete,' Jake agreed.

'John,' she countered, sure that it was John's room in which she'd spent the night. Then she remembered Tony mentioning something about Pete.

'I'm in Pete's room,' Jake said firmly, 'while my place is getting renovated.'

Tony *had* told her that, Mel suddenly realized, but he hadn't said the friend staying with him was Jake. Or that Jake looked amazing when naked and wet.

A shiver skittered across her shoulders. Naked was good, was what she'd been wanting. Not that she'd have chosen, given a choice, to pick Tony's apartment as a setting for her initiation into the mysteries of sex. But Jake was here and so was she, and except for the towel wrapped hastily around his middle, he was as ready for sex as any man could be. No reason now not to make the most of the situation.

Virile man, willing woman. Losing her virginity could be done in an instant. If only her mouth wasn't suddenly so dry.

She took a deep breath, trailed her fingers across his chest, and bestowed on him her best come-hither smile. 'Do you always wander around other people's apartments naked?'

'I wasn't exactly wandering.'

'You left the door unlocked.'

'I heard Tony go out. I didn't know anyone else was here.'

There were a lot of muscles beneath her fingers, rippling and firm and

78

entirely un-lawyer-like.

He peered into her face. 'Have you got a cramp?'

'Certainly not.' She snatched her hand away.

'You look a little funny.'

'What do you mean, funny?'

'I don't know.' He frowned. 'Perhaps a little pale.'

'Maybe I was going to kiss you,' she said, trying for a sexy, sultry voice.

'Kiss me?' he asked.

'We almost kissed before.'

'What makes you think we're going to do it now?'

'Don't you want to?' she demanded.

'The fact that I'm naked doesn't mean you can take advantage of me.'

'Take advantage?' she squeaked, all sultriness gone.

'You're the one touching me.'

'You're holding my wrist.' She tugged her hand free. Then against her volition that hand wandered also and made its way up his neck.

'What about Tony?' he asked quietly.

'Like you said. He's not here.' With trembling fingers, she caressed the soft skin at the nape of his neck.

'So that makes it all right?' Jake's voice was hard.

'Makes it easier,' she replied, shifting her other hand and touching his waist.

For an instant desire lit up his eyes, along with need and burgeoning excitement. Then Jake's eyes shuttered shut and his lips touched hers.

She'd imagined them warm, hadn't reckoned with hot, had thought they'd be soft, not hard as driving steel. She could tell he held back for his mouth scarcely moved, then his tongue tickled her lips and thrust its way past them, probing and exploring, releasing sensations.

The deeper their kiss grew, the more she wanted.

He groaned, pulled her closer and enfolded her with his arms.

Her heart pounded, went still, then pounded even more, increasing its tempo until she thought she might die.

If she did it would be a death of ecstasy, engulfed as she was in heat and light.

He pulled away. 'What about Tony?' he asked again.

'What about him?' she gasped.

Jake's dark eyes grew stern. 'Don't you care what he thinks?'

'This is none of his business.' She didn't want to think of Tony and his cousinly concerns. She was a grown woman with a grown woman's needs. She pressed her body closer. 'Forget Tony,' she said.

'I can't,' he growled, 'and you shouldn't either.'

'I already have.' She lifted her lips to his.

Why the hell had she kissed him? Jake tried to think of Tony, his friend . . . his best friend. No decent man made love to his best friend's woman. And it was only yesterday he'd made his vow, a vow not to have sex for the next two months. Now here he was, faltering at the first hurdle.

But the woman in his arms tasted of

sunlight and drops of rain on newly mown grass. She was a nymph, a woodland pixie, a siren in pale silk. She bewitched him, enticed him, turned his resolve to mush.

He broke off their kiss, wishing it was as easy to break the spell she cast. 'I didn't take you for a two-timer.'

Her eyes clouded, grew confused. 'Two-timer?' she asked.

'Tony,' he said.

Her eyes were huge and still filled with confusion, making him want to hold and protect her. He pulled in a shallow breath, tried not to let her perfume fill his nostrils, for if it did, her magic would ensnare him.

'You've gone straight from your boyfriend's bed to the arms of another man. I'd call that two-timing,' he said, with disdain.

'Boyfriend?' she said, looking even more stunned. She took a step backward, but the door blocked her way, had somehow shut behind her.

'Tony,' he repeated.

She shook her head.

In the distance, Jake heard the front door slam, but before he could figure out the significance of that sound, Tony hollered Melissa's name.

Mel jumped, turned around, her movement pressing her backwards into Jake's arms. Involuntarily, he caught her, knowing he should thrust her away. But to do so was impossible. Her body fit his as snugly as a football held in the crook of a running back's arm, and the heat of her skin sent shivers down his spine. Every breath he took in brought the perfumed scent of a woman newly risen from her bed. He groaned again.

'It's Tony,' she whispered.

'I thought you didn't care.'

'I don't care, but — ' She twisted in his arms. ' — I'd rather he not find us like this. Just keep quiet.'

He drew back, let her go. 'You should answer him.'

'No.'

'Or go out,' he suggested.

'I'm happy where I am.'

'Then I'll go out.'

'He'll see you if you do.'

He gazed at her sternly. 'I don't intend to hide in the bathroom.'

'Maybe he'll leave if he thinks we're both out.'

'Mel,' Tony called again, the sound of his voice closer.

'Answer him,' Jake demanded. Damn the woman. Damn himself too.

'No,' she persisted, her chin tilting upwards. 'Tony won't understand.'

'You should have thought of that sooner, before you flung yourself at me.'

'I didn't notice you ducking.'

'I'm not the one with a boyfriend.'

Mel's brow crinkled. 'I don't have a boyfriend?'

'Tony doesn't deserve this.'

'This has nothing to do with Tony.'

They'd been speaking in whispers, but suddenly she went completely still. Was it fear keeping her from moving? Fear Tony would hear them talking and discover their unfaithfulness.

Jake's jaw clenched. He had to push her away, had to do it for Tony and for himself also, had to extricate himself before he got embroiled with a woman he couldn't want.

'Mel,' Tony hollered, this time from the hall just outside the bathroom door. 'Are you in there?'

'She's here,' Jake said quietly. He stepped backward in an effort to create space between them, and for an instant he thought she wouldn't turn the door handle, that she'd grab the lock instead and twist it closed. But with a straightening of her shoulders, Mel opened the door.

5

'Mel!' Tony exclaimed. His gaze darted from her face then flew to Jake's, then, in an instant, back again to hers.

She couldn't see Jake move, but she felt a chill when he stepped away.

'What the hell's going on?' Tony demanded.

'Just looking for my toothbrush,' Mel said lightly. She reached past Jake toward the bathroom sink and the Cinderella toothbrush Trish had bought her as a joke. 'You're back early,' she said to Tony. 'Have you had your breakfast yet?'

Jake slid past her. 'She's hungry,' he said, casting an indecipherable glance in Mel's direction.

'She's always hungry,' Tony replied. 'But there's no food in the bathroom.'

'I am not always hungry, and Jake and I were just talking.' She gritted her teeth, furious at herself that she had explained. Never explain, Trish had once told her. Nothing aroused suspicions more.

Jake smiled at her then, cool as a cucumber, not looking guilty at all, he reached over her shoulder and grabbed his shirt and boxers.

Mel caught her breath. All that self-possession must come from years of practice.

Then Jake stepped past her and past Tony too.

'Where are you going?' her cousin demanded.

'I've got to get dressed,' Jake replied. 'Then I'll make you both breakfast.'

* * *

Mel sat on her bed and tried to still the frantic thumping of her heart. Somehow Jake had got them out of that bathroom without Tony discovering that they had kissed. A feat for which she was exceedingly grateful. The less her cousin knew, the better she liked it. She didn't want him interfering in her life.

It took skill to get anything past D'Angelo men. She had only managed it on a few occasions. She'd have to manage it now if she intended to seduce her cousin's friend, which, as the memory of Jake's lips filled her mind, she decided she'd have to do. She was no longer sixteen, but the passion was still there for her first fantasy lover.

With a sigh, she rooted in her suitcase for her jeans and a tee shirt. She had to get to the kitchen as fast as she could before Jake said something that would give them away. If Tony got any inkling of how she'd behaved, he'd ship her back to her father before she could mutter the word *virgin*!

She wiggled into her clothes and slipped on her chipmunk slippers, then, staring at her feet, took the slippers off. Not sexy, Trish would have pronounced. Fluffy slippers might be comfortable, but they definitely wouldn't entice a man to make love to her.

She would leave her feet bare. They had never looked so good. Her toenails were crimson, as were her fingernails. Both hands and feet looked as though they belonged to a model. With a smile, she added a silver ankle chain then made her way down the hall to the kitchen.

The rich scent of coffee greeted her, but was overlaid by the eye-watering smell of burning toast. She hurried to the toaster. 'Is nobody watching this?'

'I'll get it,' Jake said, trying to ignore the way his blood surged through his veins. Tony's woman, he decided, was just as sexy clothed as she had been almost naked. If she was going to be a fixture in this apartment, he was going to have to make himself scarce. For Tony's woman was *trouble* wrapped in cotton and denim.

But when he took the toast from her, when their hands almost touched, he remembered that same hand on his chest. 'Sit down,' he ordered, more gruffly than he intended. 'I'll fry us all some eggs.'

'No thanks,' Mel said.

'Great,' Tony murmured, his answer half muffled by his perusal of the paper.

Jake dropped the toast into the garbage.

'I could have scraped that,' Mel protested.

'I'll make more.' Jake dropped some butter into a frying pan, determined to keep moving, not look at her or talk.

He cracked an egg against the side of the pan. The yolk broke and smeared yellow into the white. 'Damn,' he cursed, and cracked another. This time, for the sake of his concentration, he removed Mel from his line of vision. He cracked more eggs, let them fry for a moment then flipped them over in one easy movement. He turned to Tony. 'I checked on the renovations yesterday. They're taking longer than I thought. I should probably just check into a hotel.'

'Don't even think about it, man.' Tony put his paper down. 'I haven't beaten you at basketball yet.'

Jake grinned at his friend, and slid some eggs onto his plate. 'You've been threatening to do that since I got back to Seattle. You couldn't manage it in college. What makes you think anything's changed?'

'Just name the place and time,' Tony said with enthusiasm, 'and I'll take you to the cleaners. Mel, you can referee.'

Jake's smile died. 'Seriously, man, I don't want to get in your way.'

'Way of what?' Tony asked.

'Entertaining.' Jake nodded his head in Mel's direction. 'You and your girlfriend,' he added meaningfully.

'Girlfriend!' Tony laughed. 'Mel's not my girlfriend. She's my cousin, for God's sake. Don't you remember her? She tripped all over you at that family picnic I took you to.'

'Your cousin?' Jake turned and found Mel's gaze on him, saw that her cheeks were tinged with red. 'Why didn't you tell me?' he demanded. Why the hell hadn't he seen it? He could see it now. Tony's and Mel's hair was the same color, as was the shape of their eyes. Add in the dimples on both their right cheeks and they could be brother and sister, not cousins.

'Why didn't you know?' Mel answered coolly.

'It's a long time since I met you.' Eight years, at least. It seemed longer than that.

'Not so long,' she countered.

'You were younger then.'

'So were you.'

'I was in university,' Jake said firmly. 'You were just a kid.'

'I was sixteen.' Her chin lifted as she glared at him.

'You were a pest,' Tony said, shoveling half an egg into his mouth.

Mel scowled at her cousin.

'She wasn't a pest,' Jake said quietly.

'That's not what you said then.'

Jake frowned at Tony, willing him to shut up, then glancing back at Mel, saw it was too late. The desire he'd seen in her eyes before had changed to a mixture of anger and embarrassment.

'Exactly what did you say?' she asked.

'Nothing,' Jake muttered.

'Plenty,' Tony contradicted.

'I said I thought you were cute.' He hadn't really thought much beyond that. Mel had been too young to interest him then, and he'd been too distracted by other women who were older. Although when he thought back, he did remember Mel's smile. It had warmed him back then just as it had the day before.

'Cute?' Mel repeated, in a strangled voice, and the expression on her face was growing frostier by the second.

'Cute kid, to be exact.' Tony tilted back his chair and grinned at them both.

Jake didn't have to look at Mel to see how she was reacting. He only knew he wanted to bop Tony on the nose. 'Young lady,' he corrected. 'I'm sure I said young lady.'

Mel's beautiful smile was nowhere to be seen.

With a groan, Jake turned to Tony. 'This is your fault, mate. Fix it.'

'No chance, buddy. I'm just glad she's not mad at me.' Tony ducked as Mel tossed a sugar cube at his head. 'D'Angelo women have tempers,' he explained. Another sugar cube zinged by his ear. 'Think I'll go grab a shower.' His grin widening, Tony hurried from the room.

Jake turned back to Mel, whose hand hovered too near the sugar bowl for his comfort. 'Did *you* know who *I* was when you saw me yesterday?'

'Of course,' she replied.

'So why didn't *you* say anything?' he asked again.

'There seemed no point.' Her lips pressed together. 'You gave no indication you recognized me and I didn't think we'd ever see each other again.' She looked at him through narrowed eyes. 'Then Jessie told me you called her that afternoon.'

'I wanted to talk to her,' Jake replied. 'The firm's responsible for her case.'

'Your uncle is, not you.'

'If one of your relatives creates a problem, don't you try to fix it?'

For an instant, she looked startled, then with a chuckle, she jerked her head towards the bathroom, from which emanated an off-key baritone. 'I do it all the time.'

'Exactly,' Jake said.

Mel shot him a look. 'I think you called for another reason.' She took another step towards him.

Two days earlier, he'd have taken her in his arms, but he'd made a vow and was damned well not going to break it. Mel had surprised him in the bathroom that morning. She was surprising him now. He wasn't going to let her surprise again.

'Business,' he said. 'That's all that call was.'

'Then you're helping Jessie with her case?'

'That's what I said.' He willed Mel to move away.

'I guess that means we'll be seeing a lot of each other.'

'I don't see why.' He took a step back. Her smile wasn't just warm, it was seductive as hell.

'I work for Jessie,' Mel went on, her breath caressing him with all the sweetness of perfume.

'In what capacity?' His senses demanded that he cease his hasty bet, and hold this woman in his arms as soon as possible.

'I'm her care-giver,' Mel replied. 'She's scheduled to have a hip operation in the September. Until then, she needs help around the house.'

He gazed at her thoughtfully. 'The help my mother hired never looked as good as you. They were all middle-aged and chucked me under my chin.' His brows drew together. 'Do you help clean?'

'According to Tony,' she replied, with a chuckle, 'the world as we know it would come to an end if I did. I do clean a little, but mostly I make sure Jessie gets in and out of her bath safely, eats properly, takes her medication — that sort of thing.'

'Seems a funny sort of a job for a young woman like you.' She looked like a student in her jeans and bare feet, and the shimmer of silver encircling her ankle. Even her toes looked young and carefree with some indescribably cheery color dabbed onto her nails.

'I'm not that young,' she reminded him. 'And I like what I'm doing.' She glanced at her watch. 'In fact I'd better get going. I have to be at Jessie's by eleven, and I've got an apartment I want to check out first.'

'Then you're not staying here?'

'With Tony?' She laughed. 'I'm sure he thinks I'll cramp his style.'

He should feel relieved that she was going, but all he felt was sharp regret.

'I'm moving in with a friend,' Mel went on.

'If her father approves,' Tony said

suddenly, re-appearing in the doorway with hair still wet from his shower.

'He'll approve,' Mel said firmly. She glanced at her watch. 'But I've got to get going.'

'I know I promised to take you,' Tony said, 'but I'm running late myself. How about you, Jake? Care to accompany my cousin and make sure this apartment she wants is not some den of iniquity?'

The last thing he should do was spend more time in Mel's company, but if he could handle that, Jake decided, could be with her and not want her, then he should have no trouble keeping his promise. 'Sure,' he said. 'I've got nothing on.'

*　*　*

He had made a mistake.

He was handling nothing.

When he looked at Mel, all he wanted was to touch her, to run his hands over her soft skin and hair.

'Stop here,' Mel ordered.

'Here?' Jake stared incredulously at the apartment building to his right. Mel couldn't be serious about living here. The building might be what some would call trendy, but Mel's father would no doubt label it decrepit. It rose five stories in the middle of the block and surrounding it on both sides were shops of unknown character, selling God knows what to God knows whom. Sprinkled amongst the shops were various cafés, offering international delights at cut-rate prices.

He had to admit the atmosphere of the street appealed, with its cosmopolitan air and people of every age and race. But it wasn't the sort of area for a girl like Mel, especially if she came home late any night. Why, just down the block was a distinctly shady-looking bar, and across and to the right was what looked like a pawn shop.

'Park there,' Mel said again, pointing to a space between an old Buick and a Jetta.

Jake nosed his '76 Mustang convertible in, hoping the rust off the Buick wouldn't jump the gap. He'd spent hours polishing and waxing the car his father had left him, uncomplicated hours, in the years before his father died.

He pulled the club lock from the back seat and clamped it to his steering wheel.

Mel's lips tilted up. 'You have got to be kidding?'

'Better safe than sorry in a neighborhood like this.'

'Nobody is going to steal an old car like this.'

'This car is a classic.' Jake patted the dashboard. 'Every guy I know admires it.'

'There's no need to wait if you're that worried about your car. Just drop me here and I'll make my own way to Jessie's.'

'Not on your life.' He opened his door and stepped out onto the road. 'I promised Tony I'd see you got here safely, and I always do what I promise.' He didn't add that Tony had issued another instruction in private that Jake was not to show any romantic interest in his cousin.

'I'd trust you with my life,' Tony had said when Mel was off collecting her purse from her room, 'but I know what you're like where women are concerned. I don't know what the two of you were doing in the bathroom, but if you make her fall in love with you, you're a dead man.'

Gritting his jaw, Jake moved around his car, opened Mel's door and held out his hand.

Mel took hold then stared at the hand clasping hers. How did Jake manage to keep stealing her breath? Was it his touch, or simply his male energy? Whatever it was she didn't want him coming in with her, and casting around his critical lawyer gaze. She wanted to seduce him, not get to know him, and definitely not let him see the intimate details of her life. Trish's apartment was tiny, with barely room for one woman. Jake would say there was no room for two.

'Why don't you wait in the car?' Mel suggested.

His only response was to grip her arm more tightly.

He was doing it again, was creating sensations that dislodged rational thought. Which she supposed was exactly what she'd been seeking when she made the decision to have sex at last. But she'd wanted the experience only on her terms, didn't want to regress into a giddy schoolgirl.

'There's no doorman,' Jake said, as he led her up the sidewalk. He frowned when they reached the open front door. 'And why the hell isn't this door locked?'

'It usually is.' Mel searched for the buzzer button bearing Trish's name.

'Anyone could get in.' Jake dropped her arm. Before Mel could press Trish's button, he pressed, instead, the button labeled Super.

'Yeah?' said the voice who answered the buzz.

'The door's open,' Jake growled.

'Like I promised,' the Super snapped. 'Just go on up to Suite 302 and lock the door behind you.'

Mel giggled and stepped in through the doorway.

'I could be an axe murderer,' Jake muttered, glowering in her direction. 'And that man who's supposed to be keeping his tenants safe has just let me in without checking who I was.'

'He's trusting,' Mel said, her smile widening as she spoke. 'I like that.'

'You won't like it when your apartment gets broken into.'

Mel's smile died. This wasn't how she had envisioned the process of seduction. What she wanted was nameless sex, not to have the man who appeared to be a lustful lady's perfect choice giving her advice with her own family's persistence. 'Are you sure your name's not D'Angelo?'

'What do you mean?'

'You're worse than my father, and that's saying something.' She pushed past him into the apartment's foyer. 'Come on,' she said. 'I don't have all day.'

'Why not forget the whole thing?'

'Never.' She jabbed the elevator button with her finger.

'Does it work?' he asked, eyeing the conveyance suspiciously.

'Of course.' She crossed her fingers behind her back. The last time she'd been here, it had been out of order. Due to the tenants on the top floor, Trish had explained, whose legendary parties involved overcrowding the elevator, resulting in a groaning climb upwards, then a squeaking of cogs as it came back down. The day before Mel's visit, it had finally given up the ghost, and Mel had to climb the stairs to the fourth floor.

Too bad she hadn't decided to do the same thing this time, for she'd forgotten another pertinent fact about the elevator. It was tiny, intimate, just like those in Paris. If you shared it, it meant you had to stand close.

The doors opened. They stepped inside. At once Mel felt engulfed by Jake. She remembered what Trish had said about her ex-boyfriend, and how the two had made love in an elevator like this.

Her cheeks began to burn, and the side of her body closest to Jake felt as though there were millions of exposed nerve endings.

If she were Trish, this would all be easy, but she wasn't Trish, and she'd never found anything harder.

Then, with a suddenness that shocked, the elevator creaked to a groaning stop. A sharp ding indicated the doors sliding open.

Mel tried to still her rapidly beating heart. 'This way,' she said, stepping out into the hall.

A swift glance reassured her that the nude neighbor wasn't there, and the tenant on the other side wasn't smoking by the hall window. He didn't like to smoke in his own apartment, Trish had told her, and seemed oblivious to the fact that his smoke spread throughout the building. Trish said she didn't mind for the neighbor was generous and always had a spare cup of sugar when she ran out.

Mel chuckled at the notion of her friend Trish baking, for she'd seen what she had managed when they'd both been in high school. Muffins that didn't rise, and soufflés that fell, and cookies that were best described as truly dreadful. Mel's cooking was one of the reasons Trish was glad to have her stay, for normally Trish lived off take-out and snacks.

'This way,' Mel said, leading the way to Trish's suite. She grabbed the door-knocker with trembling fingers and tapped it against the wood. Almost immediately, the door swung open.

'Here you are at last! I'd almost given you up.' Trish's eyes widened as she caught sight of Jake. 'Hello,' she said, her voice deepening a notch.

A trick she'd have to learn, Mel decided when she heard it, for it always had the effect of gathering men's attention. Strangely it didn't seem to mesmerize Jake.

'Jake Mallory, Trish.' Mel prayed her friend wouldn't say she'd already heard of him.

'Pleased to meet you,' Trish said then glanced at Mel, her gaze innocent. 'Did you take the stairs, Mel?' she asked. 'You look a little flushed.'

With what she hoped was a squelching look, Mel strode past her friend into the apartment.

'Mel didn't tell me she was bringing you along, Jake,' she heard Trish murmur.

Mel closed her eyes and counted to ten. 'Jake's staying with Tony and kindly offered me a lift.'

'How nice,' Trish said. 'But I feel like I've heard your name before.'

Mel shot Trish another look. If her friend said anything about what they'd discussed in the café, she would permanently disown her.

'Aren't you the lawyer for Jessie Parker?' Trish asked, keeping her gaze averted from Mel's.

'I am,' said Jake. 'At least I am now.'

'Well, I'm pleased to meet you.' Trish turned at last back to Mel. 'But I'm afraid I've got to go. I'll leave you to look around by yourselves. I've got dry cleaning to pick up and then I'm out to lunch. Just lock up when you go, Mel. I've put a set of keys for you on the kitchen table.'

Kitchen table was a misnomer. There was no way any furniture would fit in the kitchen. Trish's table and chairs took up a corner of the living room, leaving a sofa to tuck into the bay window and a couple of easy chairs to form wings out the side. A comfortable room, Mel had always thought. She smiled her thanks at Trish, but sighed with relief when her friend headed out the door.

'Small,' Jake commented, once Trish had shut the door behind her.

'Cozy,' Mel replied. 'Sit down. I'll just be a moment.'

'Checking out your room?'

'Yes,' she said, frowning.

'Lead on,' he said.

'I don't need a second opinion.'

'In my experience women always need a second opinion.'

She could see he was joking, but despite his smile, she was suddenly afraid. She was attracted to Jake, had imagined making love to him and would love him to be her one-night stand. But perhaps it was better to find a stranger for no-strings sex, not a man like Jake whom she knew and liked.

Yet strangers were scarce, might even be dangerous. If only she was more experienced at such games. Trish would tell her to stop worrying if she was here, and to make love to Jake right there in the living room, get rid of the virginity burden once and for all.

Even her grandmother had always said there was no time like the present.

Although, at no moment in Nona's life would her grandmother have been referring to no-strings sex.

Mel frowned. She couldn't do it. Not here. Not now. She wasn't like Trish. She needed more time. She needed a plan. 'This way,' she said, leading Jake down the hall.

She'd only once seen the room Trish had suggested she occupy, and it didn't stand out hugely in her memory. All she recalled was that it had a bed, a bed Trish was storing for her brother and his wife until they got back in September from their honeymoon trip to Europe.

But when she opened the door at the end of the hall, Mel found the room itself had a charm all its own. With its aquamarine curtains and antique dresser, and a bunch of red tulips in front of the window.

Surely they were out of season, especially for Seattle, who held the country's record for early spring weather. The tulips, however, created

110

the perfect impression, injected a warmth just right for a couple making love for the first time.

Mel's step faltered.

Jake bumped up against her. 'Is this the room?' he asked, his breath caressing her neck as he leaned forward to see.

Flustered, uncertain, Mel simply nodded. Then, taking a deep breath, she stepped inside.

Her gaze was pulled immediately towards the bed, and the colorful quilt covering its surface, a quilt that looked as though it had once covered real lovers, who had probably been together the whole of their lives. She remembered Trish had talked about buying an antique quilt, one she'd found on a trip to Pennsylvania. Trish might work in marketing and know what was chic, but she still had a streak of romance in her soul.

'How much stuff do you have?' Jake asked, moving towards the window.

'Not much,' Mel answered, following.

'Good thing,' Jake said. 'This room is already full.'

'Trish is a packrat, and she's always doing favors for her friends.' Mel ran her tongue over suddenly dry lips. 'She's storing that bed for her brother who's away.'

Jake had tried his damnedest to keep his gaze *off* the bed, for when he looked at it, he thought of making love, and when he thought of making love, he thought of Mel.

Jenny would be laughing if she could see him now, would already be plotting how to spend her extra wages, as well as figuring out which friend of his she could ensnare.

'It's hot in here,' he said, swiping his hand around the inside of his collar. 'Let's open the window.' He refused to believe the heat was coming from Mel. He'd known a thousand girls more attractive than her, but something about her drew him to her. She was making it damned hard to stay at arm's length.

Especially when she looked at him as she was doing now, with her head on an angle and her tongue licking her lips.

He needed some air. He tugged at the window in an attempt to get it open, found it stiff with crusted white paint. When he finally succeeded in creating a crack, he bent low and breathed deep. He couldn't believe he'd been reduced to this. He'd thought it would be easy to stay away from women, hadn't known it would be like fighting a guerrilla war, where at any moment, a bomb could go off.

His heart was beating too fast in his chest, and his skin felt damp with sudden sweat. He had the sensation of fight or flight, but when he looked at Mel, he knew he couldn't flee.

With a silent groan, he straightened. Mel's hand touched his on the narrow window ledge, and her eyes were half closed as though to shut out the light. Her skin had the faintest touch of moisture on its surface, like dew on a flower in the early morning. It gave off a perfume just as sweet. 'Seen enough?' he asked.

'Almost.' She turned to face him. 'When you kissed me in the bathroom — '

'It was you who kissed me.'

'We kissed each other.'

'Maybe.' All he knew was that it took all of his strength to stop himself from kissing her now.

'I thought perhaps you'd like to finish what we started.'

'That's not a good idea. Tony wouldn't like it.' And from the way her lips were trembling, it seemed as though kissing was the last thing she wanted.

'I don't care what Tony likes.'

She moved closer. They almost touched. Jake pulled back. Was she doing this on purpose? Had Jenny somehow roped Mel into sabotaging his bet?

Impossible. Even Jenny wasn't that sneaky. All he had to do was exert self-control. All Mallory men had self-control aplenty.

Then Mel lifted her arms and put them around his neck, pulling him towards her until their lips touched. Jake remembered too late that in the past his self-control hadn't extended to resisting women.

She tasted different this time, but just as nice, was soft and moist and tantalizingly tangy. Then her tongue touched his and desire snaked through him, making for his loins in a lightning attack.

His arms crept around her. His hands slid beneath her shirt. Her skin was like satin, he thought dazedly. Then she moaned and the sound brought him to his senses.

He had to stop, put on the brakes, not just for him, but for both their sakes. Then another moan from Mel's lips erased all thoughts of stopping. He buried his face against her neck. She smelled and looked wonderful, felt wonderful, too, as though she had bathed in warm milk before a fire and the milk had turned her body into cream.

'Make love to me,' she whispered, then in a strangled voice said, 'Let's have sex.'

Some part of his brain snapped free of the dream that seemed to be playing with him as the star.

Sex wasn't an option. Wasn't that what he'd promised? It was a struggle to remember exactly what he had vowed.

'We'd better go,' he answered hoarsely, not sure that he could.

Her hand rested against his neck, her desire tangible through her touch, fueling the desire he felt for her also. Words of retraction sprang to his lips, but with great will, he held them in.

He didn't want this passion to end, no longer felt an experienced lover, but with an effort that hurt with a physical pain, he took a step backward away from her magic.

The minute Jake moved, Mel felt his loss, couldn't believe he had rejected what she offered. Trish had said it was easy to take a man to bed, but nothing about this man was easy. He didn't want her, despite her thinking that he did. Now he had refused her in no uncertain terms.

Trish would have laughed and made a joke, would somehow have managed to retain her composure. Mel felt like crying and running away, but she lifted her chin, and stared into Jakes eyes. 'You're right,' she said. 'It's time to go.'

'Go where?' he demanded.

'Don't worry,' she said scathingly, 'I'm not going to tell Tony.'

'There's nothing to tell. And I don't give a damn who you tell what.'

His words hit her as hard as a smack to the head.

She turned her back to him and stopped her body from trembling by reciting the periodic table in her head. One day soon Jake Mallory would get down on his knees, would want her so much he would beg for sex.

6

She should have told him no when he offered to drive her to Jessie's, for then she would have had a cross-town bus trip to think out a plan to change Jake's mind.

'Thanks for the lift,' she said stiffly, when at last they arrived at Jessie's white Spanish-style house.

'You're welcome,' he replied, getting out of the car too.

'Where are you going?' she demanded.

'Thought I'd come in.' With a wave of his arm, he gestured for her to precede him up the walk.

'There's no need,' she said firmly, not moving one inch. 'I'm here to work. I told you that. I'm not leaving until much later. I won't need a ride.'

'I'm here to visit Ms. Parker.'

She stared at him, incredulous. 'Why didn't you tell me that before?' Why didn't he feel as awkward as she? He was going about his day as though nothing had happened.

Perhaps for him, nothing had.

Perhaps that's what separated men from women, what she'd have to understand if she intended to proceed. She'd paid lip service in her mind as to how she would do things, how easy it would be to complete the act of sex. But she'd reckoned without the differences arising between the sexes, would have to factor those in if she was going to succeed.

'I told you I was following through with Ms. Parker's case,' Jake said, not seeming at all perturbed.

'You didn't tell me you intended to visit her today.'

'That was a spur of the moment decision.'

She regarded him thoughtfully. Maybe he *had* felt something. Maybe he was as reluctant as her to leave things as they were. Maybe he didn't know, or was afraid to admit, just how much he wanted and desired her.

Another characteristic of men she had read about in books. They didn't always know what they wanted when they had it.

Slowly, she led Jake up Jessie's sidewalk, aware of him as he followed close behind. Was he staring at her head or keeping his gaze lower? Deliberately, she added a wiggle to her walk.

'You all right?' he asked. 'Does your hip hurt or something?'

'I'm fine,' she said, tossing back her hair, hoping he'd catch a whiff of her new Mayan Wave shampoo, which supposedly embodied the scent of the Caribbean ocean and the mysterious allure of ancient Indian races.

'Jesus,' he said, 'there's something in my eye. A speck of dust or something.'

With a smile, she turned around. Then her smile died. He was eight feet behind, too far to have become entranced by the effects of her hair. With a sigh, she walked back and put her hand to his chin.

'Let me see,' she said, tilting his face up to the light.

'Not so rough,' he complained.

'Don't be a baby.'

Her fingertips began to tingle, rendering them numb and increasingly clumsy. She gritted her teeth. Fine doctor she'd be if she couldn't control her reaction when touching a man.

One more reason to get some experience with the opposite sex.

'It's nothing,' Jake insisted. He jerked his head away.

'Keep still,' she ordered, pulling him back.

She ran her finger up his cheek, caught her breath when he caught his, felt the heat beneath her hand and almost let go. Throat muscles tightening, she reached his eye.

'Let it go loose,' she instructed.

'Let what go loose?'

She noticed then what she hadn't noticed before, that his shoulders were tense and so was his jaw.

'Your eyelid,' she said. 'I'm going to

pull the top lid down over the bottom.'

'And just what do you hope to achieve by that?'

'Whatever's in your eye will get scraped out.'

He flinched, his expression suddenly that of a little boy's.

She chuckled and said, 'Just hold still.' Slowly, carefully, she took hold of his top eyelid by holding firmly to his eyelashes. 'Is it loose?' she murmured.

'As loose as it's ever going to be.'

Slowly she pulled the eyelid down and over the bottom lashes. 'Just breathe,' she instructed. 'It's not as though you're giving birth.'

'Thank God for that.'

She could kiss him again. It would be so easy. She could do it before he ever knew what hit him. But she didn't want that. She wanted him to beg.

'Mel,' a voice called from the house behind her.

Mel twirled around, her cheeks flaring hot. Jake's eyelid snapped back unattended.

'Hi Jessie,' Mel said.

'Didn't mean to interrupt,' the old woman called out. 'I didn't know you and your friend were saying your good-byes.'

'We're not saying good-bye,' Mel denied.

Jake moved past her and held out his hand. 'It's a pleasure to meet you at last, Ms. Parker. I'm Jake Mallory, your attorney.'

'So you're the young man I've been hearing so much about.'

Jake glanced back at Mel, his eyes amused.

'Not so much,' she said, casting a pleading look at Jessie.

The old woman seemed not to notice. 'I didn't realize you and Mel were dating.'

'We're not,' Mel explained. 'Jake had something in his eye. I was helping get it out.'

'That's not what we called it in my day,' Jessie said. Then she turned in the doorway. 'Come along, now, come

123

along.' She led the way down the hall, leaning heavily on her cane.

Jake stood aside so Mel could go first. She did so carefully, not wanting to touch him, not wanting to fall again under his spell.

'How's your eye now?' Jessie asked Jake as soon as she had lowered herself onto a kitchen chair.

'Fine,' Jake assured her. 'I had a good nurse.'

'Better get her while she's cheap. Soon enough she'll be charging you for her attentions.'

'What do you mean?' Jake asked.

Mel stared at her hands. Why on earth had Jessie worded things as she had? From the way she spoke, Jake would probably think she was a hooker.

'Didn't Mel tell you?' Jessie's eyebrows rose. 'In a few years' time this young lady will be a doctor.'

She hadn't wanted Jessie either to tell Jake the truth, for sharing dreams and lives only brought people closer, a situation incompatible with sex with no strings.

'No,' Jake said slowly, turning to Mel. 'She told me she was your care-giver.'

'She is at the moment, but come September she's going to medical school. She won't have time to look after me then.'

'I'll always have time for you,' Mel said swiftly, 'but by then you won't need me like you do now. You'll have had your operation and be getting around fine.'

'So long,' Jessie said, regarding Mel with affection, 'that being well doesn't stop you from coming to see me.'

'Nothing will stop that!'

'Although,' Jessie went on spiritedly, 'I might be too busy. Did I tell you I'm planning a trip to Vegas?'

'Vegas!' Mel exclaimed, then she began to chuckle. She'd miss people like Jess if she became a surgeon as she planned, for she loved the way they never failed to surprise.

'A doctor,' Jake repeated, harking

back to what Jessie had previously said. 'Why didn't you tell me?' he asked Mel.

'It didn't come up.' She flung her hair back over her shoulder.

'Mel's grandmother would have been so proud,' Jessie went on.

Mel shifted uncomfortably from one foot to the other. 'Jake doesn't want to hear what my grandmother would have liked.'

'On the contrary,' Jake said, 'I want to know everything about you.'

'You came here to see Jess.'

'Don't worry about me.' Jessie waved her cane in the air. 'I've got plenty of time.'

'Well, I don't,' Mel said. 'I need to help you with your exercises. The doctor said you should be doing them every morning.'

'The doctor says a lot of things. That doesn't mean we have to listen.'

'Jessie,' Mel said sternly.

'The girl's a taskmaster,' Jessie complained, but she got to her feet. 'Come along, Mr. Mallory. I've got the papers you wanted to see in my study.'

'Jake. Call me Jake.'

'When did you ask for papers?' Mel demanded.

'The other day,' he replied. 'After you left my office.'

'He phoned me,' Jessie said, smiling slyly at Mel, 'and asked about you.'

A burst of pleasure shot through Mel, pleasure that intensified when she saw Jake's discomfort.

'This way, young man,' Jessie ordered, slowly moving toward the door. 'I'll show you to the study.'

Mel stared after the two, suddenly worried what Jessie would say next. Dear as the old woman was, she had a tendency to meddle, and she always thought she knew what was best.

With a sigh, Mel moved toward the sink and filled the kettle with water. Then she turned her attention to preparing Jessie's lunch. Her elderly friend always said she wasn't hungry then she nibbled on crackers and called it a meal. Jessie needed her strength, for her operation as much as anything else.

'He's good-looking,' Jessie said, startling Mel as she suddenly shuffled back into the kitchen. The old woman dropped again onto a solid maple chair and hung her cane from the basket of a low-hanging spider fern. 'No wonder you came back from his office all flustered.'

'I wasn't flustered!' Mel protested.

'Tall, dark and handsome, they'd have said in my day. Your Jake Mallory is gorgeous.'

'He's not *my* Jake Mallory.'

'Then why were you canoodling on my front lawn?'

'Canoodling!' Mel exclaimed. 'I don't even know what that means!'

Jessie chuckled, then, pushing aside the fern foliage, reached for something in the depths of the planter pot. Her hand emerged clutching a pack of cigarettes.

'I certainly hope,' Mel said sternly, 'that you're not intending to light one of those. You know what the doctor said.' But she didn't hold out much hope that Jessie would listen to the doctor. She'd seen the elderly woman breathe deeply as they passed through the puffers outside the front entrance of St. Jude's Bingo hall sucking in the smoke she was forbidden.

With an audible sigh, Jessie kept the package closed.

Mel's shoulders relaxed. In the two months Jessie had needed part-time home help, three care workers had begun work, then quit. Mel was the fourth and intended to be the last, at least until she had to stop work in the fall.

Jessie gave a hard time to anyone who tried to help her, but that stemmed from a desire for complete independence.

'Canoodling,' Jessie went on now, with a cross look at Mel, 'is kissing, necking — '

'I was simply getting a piece of dirt out of his eyes!'

'That's not what it looked like from up on the porch.'

Mel could feel perspiration form on her brow. If Jessie could only see what was in Mel's head, the old lady wouldn't be worrying about a little kiss. Mel moved to the fridge and opened the door, letting the cool air waft over her hot skin. She took her time removing the milk and prayed that her discomfiture would disappear.

'I'd snap him up if I was you, girl,' Jessie went on.

With reluctance, Mel turned to face her. 'I thought you said you didn't like lawyers.' She closed the fridge door with her foot and carried the milk and teacups over to the table.

'It was his uncle I didn't like. Jake has been more than helpful.'

She shouldn't be surprised Jessie was already calling Jake by his first name, but it felt as though this man she barely knew was infiltrating himself into every corner of her life. Not a good thing if she was going to love him and leave him.

'No milk for me,' Jessie added,

frowning at the jug in Mel's hand.

'You need the calcium,' Mel protested automatically. 'The doctor said — '

'I don't care what that young pup has to say. I've always drunk my coffee black.' Jessie selected a chocolate from the pottery dish on the table. 'I suppose you're going to tell me chocolate's bad too?' She popped a maple nut cream into her mouth.

'Chocolate's never bad.' Mel grinned as she, too, chose a chocolate, a pecan caramel, which was what she liked best. She waited in anticipation for it to soften in her mouth.

'Good girl,' Jessie said approvingly. 'Now what about this boyfriend?'

'There is no boyfriend. I told you that.' Mel moved back toward the counter as the kettle began to sing.

'I'll bet he likes a little meat on a woman's bones,' Jessie went on.

'I don't care what he likes,' Mel said irritably. 'Let's just drop it.' The last thing she wanted was Jake to hear them talking.

'A pretty girl like you! If he isn't your boyfriend now, he soon will be,' Jessie predicted.

'I have no time for boyfriends.' All she wanted was a lover, but *that* was not something she intended to share with Jessie.

'You have to make time,' Jessie replied firmly. 'At the very least, take a lover.'

Mel stared at Jessie, stunned. Were her intentions that apparent to all and sundry? Her hand holding the kettle began to shake. She put out her other hand to steady it as she poured boiling water into the tea pot. 'I thought you were off men,' she said, determined to buy some time.

'Not men,' Jessie replied, the corners of her eyes crinkling. 'Just Tom Preston. But I don't want to talk about him. I want to talk about you and Jake.'

'There's nothing to say.' It was bad enough that her girlfriend, Trish, worried about Mel's no-man status. She didn't want Jessie getting in on the act. 'How's your hip this morning?' she asked hurriedly.

'I can't complain,' Jessie said.

She seldom did complain. Mel's irritation faded. But she could tell from the puffiness below the older woman's eyes and the way her white hair had escaped its bun, that Jessie's night had been rough. The sooner she got her new hip, the better.

'And I certainly wouldn't be complaining if Jake Mallory were after me,' Jessie went on.

'Jake's not after me,' Mel protested.

'He's going to make some lucky woman a wonderful lover.'

She should have known it would be impossible to distract Jessie from the topic. She always clung to the subject of Mel's private life with the tenacity of a wartime news correspondent.

'Have you ever had one, girl?' Jessie asked suddenly.

'That's none of your business!'

'Working too hard,' Jessie went on, 'is no way to get a man.'

'I don't work all the time, and I don't want a man.'

'I'm not suggesting you get married.'

'Then you're different from my father.'

Jessie snorted back a chuckle. 'I'm merely suggesting you take a lover.'

'What's this about lovers?'

Mel spun around. Jake stood against the door jamb, his hands filled with papers.

'We were just discussing the pros and cons,' Jessie explained innocently. 'What do you think, Jake?'

He shifted his feet. 'I'm not sure what you mean.'

'Mel works too hard,' Jessie explained. 'She doesn't leave enough time for a social life.'

'Jessie!' Mel protested.

Jake shot her an amused glance. 'I would have thought your job left you ample time for dating.'

'It's not her job,' Jessie went on, 'that slows her down.'

'I'm right here, Jess,' Mel broke in. 'I

134

can speak for myself.'

'It's her studying,' Jessie continued, ignoring Mel. 'She studies too hard.'

'She'll have to study hard if she plans to be a doctor,' Jake commented.

'A surgeon!' Jessie corrected him proudly.

'A surgeon?' Jake repeated. He looked again at Mel. 'That'll take even longer.'

'I keep telling her to forget studying over the summer. What she needs is to celebrate.'

'Jess,' Mel protested.

'By taking a lover?' Jake's lips twisted into a grin.

'A date would do nicely to begin with,' Jessie said practically. 'Perhaps *you'd* like to take her out?'

Mel prayed that the floor would open up and swallow her. Then she wouldn't have to see the grin on Jake's face and know that her embarrassment had put it there. 'I can handle my own dates.' She bit her cheek. 'And so can Jake.'

'Then you're made for each other,'

Jessie replied cheerfully.

'Come on Jake, it's time you left.' Mel grabbed him by the arm and tried to tug him in the direction of the front door but, to her surprise, she couldn't budge him an inch. Surely he wanted to escape as much as she?

'How about dinner?' he asked, in a quiet voice.

'That's more like it,' Jessie said, with open approval.

Mel dropped his arm, was suddenly aware that her throat had constricted. Since talking to Trish, her plan had been to seduce the attractive Mr. Mallory, but she'd never intended to do so under the watchful eyes of Jess.

'Well, girl,' her elderly friend prompted now, 'what do you say?'

'Not tonight,' Mel replied. Perhaps one part of Trish's advice was lacking. All the magazines she'd read talked of making the man wait, getting him so lathered up, he'd be putty in her hands when the time for sex finally came.

'Tomorrow?' Jake suggested.

'Monday,' Mel replied. 'I'll have moved into the city by then.'

'So you're actually going to move into that cubbyhole?'

'Yes,' she said. 'It's exactly what I want.'

Maybe not exactly, but it would do.

'It's your funeral,' Jake said. 'I'll pick you up at eight.'

Mel stared into his eyes and straightened her shoulders. 'I'll have dinner with you, but I want to cook.'

7

Jake groaned. 'The last time I let a woman cook for me, we ended up in bed before we even started on the appetizers.'

'Tell her I'll buy the groceries,' Jenny replied.

'Don't gloat. It's not becoming.'

'I'm just trying to decide what I'll do with my extra pay.' The smile tilting Jenny's lips exploded into a grin. 'By this time tomorrow, I should be hundreds of dollars richer.'

Jake groaned again, and dropped his head into his hands.

'And let's not forget,' his assistant went on, prying his fingers one by one from his face, 'about the gorgeous man you'll have to introduce me to.'

'What about Ted?' Best to dissuade Jenny of any illusions she might hold of his matchmaking abilities.

'We agreed on a hunk,' she told him sternly, 'not a man who lives with his mother and plays bingo in the middle of the night.'

'He won a trip to Portland last month.'

Jenny narrowed her eyes and fixed Jake with her look. The look that told him she meant to collect on this bet, as she had on most of the bets they'd made over the years.

He had never figured out how she did it, how she unerringly guessed how things would turn out. She always explained airily that it was women's intuition, but even with some sort of crazy sixth sense, no one could be that lucky. At least no man he'd ever known was.

This time he was determined Jenny would lose. The others hadn't mattered, but this one did.

He wanted a woman, but he wanted to really know her, to have her as a friend before making love to her. To achieve that he had to take his time with a relationship, had to call a halt if things went too far too fast.

He could do it. He was a man. Men could do anything they set their minds to.

'You'll go on this date,' Jenny went on, 'and your resolve will turn to mush. She'll smile and you'll melt. She'll draw near and your arms will reach out. She'll pop an olive in your mouth and you'll wish it was her tongue.'

Jake drew himself up and gazed at Jenny sternly. 'I can handle it,' he said.

'Might as well give up now.'

'Maybe it's Roger you'd like to date.' He noted, with satisfaction, the smile fade from her face.

'Not Roger,' she begged.

'He's rich, handsome; he meets all the criteria.'

'He's a bore,' Jenny declared. 'No amount of money can make up for that.'

'He's not so bad.'

'Maybe not to a man. You probably enjoy talking about how the Mariners are doing, or who's the first pick in the NBA draft. But trust me, no woman wants to chat about such things.'

Perfect, Jake thought. Jenny had just provided him with the solution he'd been seeking. When things got hot, when Mel's body in his arms tested his self-control, he'd talk about sports and the heat between them would cool.

He smiled at his assistant. 'A new client came in last week while you were at the dentist. Scott Baxter is his name. He's pleasant, good-looking, has a very good job, and he didn't mention one word about any kind of sports.'

Jenny stared at him, suspicion in her eyes. 'There must be something wrong with him.'

Jake shook his head. 'Nothing,' he replied.

'You're up to something,' she accused. Then her eyes widened. 'Have you already lost our bet?'

'Of course not,' he scoffed, but in his mind he had lost it a dozen times over. Lucky for him, his mind didn't count.

'You haven't told me who's cooking this meal for you. It's been only three days since I saw you last. Even you couldn't have met someone so soon.'

Her gaze probed his, seemed to penetrate his brain.

He looked away.

She sucked in a breath.

With a sinking heart, he turned back, knowing she had figured it out.

'It's that woman who came in for Ms. Parker on Friday,' Jenny said excitedly. 'I don't believe this! She was here when you got the phone call from Tammy!'

When he'd been with Mel, he had thought of Tammy, and how, together, they had almost created a baby. It wasn't the thought of the baby that appalled, but the thought of having it with someone he didn't love. He couldn't bear to do that to a child of his.

Which was the prime reason he had to keep Mel at arm's length. If he wanted a baby, a wife, a family, he couldn't have sex with a woman he barely knew. He had to keep his bet, had to take things slowly, had to fall in love before making love.

'I'm right, aren't I?' Jenny persisted.

'I'm doing work for her employer,' Jake explained. 'I'm bound to bump into her.'

'When did you see Ms. Parker?' Jenny demanded.

'Saturday,' he admitted.

'On the weekend!' A stunned expression appeared in his assistant's eyes. 'Since when do you see clients on the weekend?'

'I have from time to time.'

'I was here Saturday morning. I'd have seen Ms. Parker if she'd come in to the office.'

'I went to her house,' he replied.

'Since when do you go to a client's house?'

Seldom, Jake thought. Almost never was more truthful. Turning his back on Jenny, he pretended to get something out of his desk drawer. 'Scott Baxter is going to be in again this morning,

Jenny. You probably want to go comb your hair or something.' He risked a swift glance in her direction.

Jenny stuck out her tongue as she had when they were kids, but despite that action her hand stole up to fluff her bangs. 'So,' she asked slowly, lowering her hand, 'are you throwing in the towel? Because if you are,' she added, 'I might need an hour or two off work.'

'To do what?' Jake asked.

'This and that,' she said mysteriously. She moved toward the door. 'I might go shopping.'

'I wouldn't spend anything just yet.' Jake drew himself up, put on his most confident expression. 'Melissa D'Angelo and I are *not* about to have sex.'

* * *

Mel punched the blue, satin-covered pillow then placed it carefully against the Indian throw rug on Trish's couch. The couch nestled in the corner of the room, looking casual, yet elegant. Mel's lips turned down. No point in kidding herself that anything in this room looked elegant. It did, however, have character and charm. That would have to be enough.

Might even make lovemaking easier to initiate. She was young, hot and single. Having sex was her right. She only hoped Jake felt the same way.

No doubt he was used to slightly older women, who played the mating game with more experience than she. But she'd watched movies and read books, had dated enough to understand how it worked. She just had to pretend when the moment came that she was experienced in matters of the heart.

Not the heart, she sternly reminded herself. This lovemaking would have nothing to do with the heart. It would be quick, a swift coupling to end the burden she carried.

She glanced around the room, wanting nothing to go wrong, then realized, with a start, that she'd forgotten the candles. She'd better set them out now so she could light them quickly when it came time to doing the deed.

She walked swiftly to her bedroom and found them where she'd left them. She took the wax tapers from her bag on her dressing table and carefully placed a couple on her dresser, then three shorter candles on the windowsill and four on the table next to her bed. Another few in the living room and all would be well.

Funky, sexy, modern and experienced. The candles said it all, she decided, with a smile. They even smelled as though they were already lit.

Then the recognizable odor of burning garlic and butter clearly penetrated her bedroom's solid wooden walls.

'Trish!' she hollered, running from the room. She slid on her stocking feet down the hall toward the kitchen.

'I think this is done,' Trish said when she arrived, looking worriedly up from the congealed mess in the frying pan.

Mel snatched the pan off the burner and gazed despairingly at the blackened butter. 'It's not done, it's ruined! Were you watching this like you promised?'

'I didn't take my eyes off it.'

'Did you turn the burner up?'

'Just a touch,' her friend admitted.

With a groan, Mel jiggled the pan this way and that, but it didn't make the burned mess disappear. 'Butter has to be melted slowly,' she explained, wishing she hadn't succumbed to Trish's offer of help. She knew her friend had only offered in order to be present when Jake arrived, for Trish had always had zero culinary expertise. Any attempt in the past she'd ever made at cooking had always ended in disaster.

But if she hadn't let Trish cook, her friend would have shadowed her around the apartment inundating her with advice. She'd had enough advice. She wanted to do this her own way.

'I promised I'd phone Ken before he went out,' Trish said. She bit her lower lip. 'I thought the food would get done faster if I turned up the heat.'

Mel shook her head, and expelled a gust of air. She was starting to feel nauseous, and there was a lump in her stomach that felt like lead. She'd have to do everything over again. She stared at the blackened butter in the pan and wished she'd stuck to one of her grandmother's recipes rather than deciding on pepper steak with béarnaise sauce. Trish had convinced her that men preferred meat over pasta and would finish the meal feeling hungry for love.

She'd wanted the sauce made before Jake got to the apartment, ready to pour over the grilled steaks. Wanted the salad made, also, and the table set, the cabernet sauvignon airing, and herself unflustered and ready for sex. She glanced at her watch. Jake would be here any minute and she wasn't ready at all. The first thing she had to do was get rid of Trish.

Her friend leaned against the counter, appearing as immovable as a stone statue.

'I'm looking forward to meeting this lawyer of yours again.'

'Another time maybe.' Mel tipped the butter down the garborator and ran hot water into the pan.

'No time like the present.' Trish took off her apron and folded it over a chair.

'You promised you'd go out!'

'Don't worry,' her friend said. 'I won't get in your way. I'll just say hello, check him out properly, then leave you two alone.'

'He'll take one look at you and fancy you madly, and that'll be the end of romance for me.'

Trish laughed and shook back her fiery hair. 'Since when,' she asked, 'has that ever happened?'

'Johnny Parker in tenth grade.'

'All he ever wanted was to help my brother soup up that junk heap of a car he had. He kept going on about the gears in the rear.' Trish rolled her eyes. 'Johnny figured going out with me would net him access to the engine.'

Mel chuckled and shook her head.

'The way I remember it is I was plucking up the courage to talk to Johnny, hoping against hope that he'd ask me to the school dance, then down the hall you wiggled and he asked you instead.'

'You missed nothing,' Trish insisted. 'He danced like a wet dishrag.' Her expression grew shrewd. 'Jake Mallory doesn't resemble anything like a damp cloth.'

Mel's belly fluttered. She glanced at her watch again. 'You've got to go *now*.' She turned Trish around and gave her a push towards the door. 'I'm nervous enough already without you giving Jake the third degree.'

'Someone has to make sure his intentions aren't honorable.'

Mel chuckled, but scooped up Trish's purse from where it sat on the table next to the door. She hung it over her friend's neck.

'If I have to stay out all night,' Trish complained, 'I should at least get to pack a bag.'

'Nobody said anything about all night. Just give me until midnight. It'll be all over by then.'

'You make it sound as though you're facing a firing squad.' Trish's blue eyes gazed sympathetically into Mel's. 'Having sex is supposed to be fun.'

'I'm sure it will be. But once I've done it once, the pressure will be off. It won't matter if I don't have it again for a long time.'

'So you're planning to have sex then tell Jake he's no longer required?'

'Something like that.' Mel bit her lip. Once she and Jake had sex, it probably would be best if she never saw him again. Hopefully, he would be relieved. From what she understood, guys were only too happy to have sex with a woman then get clean away before the woman talked commitment.

She tried to will away the worries in her head. It would all turn out fine. She and Jake would have fun and then Jake would leave. No tears, no recriminations, no commitment, no regret.

'Don't worry,' she said, twisting the door knob to the right. 'Just go!' she urged, opening the front door.

'Whoa!' Jake said, leaping to one side to avoid Trish's forward movement. 'I hadn't even knocked yet.' He stood there before them, tall and amazing-looking, exuding enough sex appeal to sweep any woman off her feet.

There would be no sweeping, Mel told herself sternly, just ordinary sex, just something to proclaim her no longer a virgin.

She fought a sudden gust of despair. When she looked at Jake, she wanted all that he had; his body, his touch, his electricity, and charisma. She wanted to be engulfed with passion and sensation, to understand truly what having sex was all about.

'Nice to meet you again.' Trish's eyes gleamed with approval. 'Mel told me you were coming over.'

'What else has she told you?' Jake cast a piercing glance directly at Mel.

Her feet seemed suddenly frozen to

the spot, and her heart, normally thudding at a slow, steady pace, now beat against her chest with painful force. Perhaps it was the adrenalin rush of getting Trish gone or the frenzy of the past two hours preparing for this date, but the air in her lungs seemed inexplicably to disappear.

'Nothing,' she replied, mustering composure. 'I've told her nothing.' She glared at Trish. 'There's nothing to tell.'

'The night's young,' Trish said gaily.

'Trish is just leaving.' Mel fixed on her friend her best commanding look.

'There's no rush,' Trish protested. 'I could sit and chat with Jake while you finish making dinner.'

'Trish,' Mel said warningly.

'All right.' Her friend laughed. 'I'm leaving. I'm leaving.'

Mel ushered Jake in, then slipped past him into the hall for a swift moment with Trish.

'He's very cute,' her friend whispered, 'but dangerously sexy. Do you think you're up to handling that?'

'Nothing easier,' Mel lied.

'Well, there's nothing like a bad boy to get the juices flowing.' Trish gave Mel an excited pinch on her arm. 'I want to hear all about it when I get home.'

'There might be nothing to tell.'

'Shall I stay and give you pointers?' Trish glanced back at Jake and gave him a wink.

'I can manage,' Mel said, as Jake grinned back.

'Just don't lose your nerve. If I had my first time to do over again, I'd definitely choose someone like your Jake.'

'He's not my Jake.' Although since she had met him when only sixteen, she had always thought of him like that. It felt as though she'd known him the whole of her life as her fantasy dream man, her lover come true.

So why was it now that the time had come, she suddenly felt afraid to continue?

'Get going,' Mel begged. Perhaps

once Trish was gone, the pressure would be off, and she could proceed at her own pace, play everything by ear.

'Bye girlfriend,' Trish said, then waved gaily to Jake. 'Nice seeing you again, Jake. Hope to see you again soon.' In the next instant she was gone, leaving behind only the scent of her perfume.

Leaving Mel alone with Jake.

The apartment suddenly seemed too small and the man beside her too big. The air between them crackled with sexual energy, threatening to fry her alive.

Jake peeled off his sweater and tossed it over one end of the sofa. 'It smells good in here.'

A drop of moisture dripped down Mel's brow. The day was hot and she'd been cleaning, but she knew in her gut that this heat had arisen from something else entirely.

Jake was clad in a tee shirt that hugged his chest and his jeans fit snugly around his hips, drawing her gaze to dangerous places. If her plan to have sex went as planned, those were places she would shortly have to explore.

With a flutter of panic, she looked into his eyes and was stunned to find they were dangerous too.

'That smell is not good,' she corrected him hoarsely, glad to have something else to concentrate on. 'What you smell is burnt butter.'

'Garlic, too.' He sniffed the air. 'Reminds me of my mother's cooking. Not that cooking was something she did very often.'

Talking about his mother should not be sexy, but maybe it didn't matter what words fell from his lips. All she knew was that she'd felt them once on her own, and all she wanted now was to feel them again.

Catching her breath, she stepped away.

The science books she had read discussed sex from a clinical point of view, an experiment in physical relations, nothing more. But the pheromones now invading her body told a different story.

'Didn't your mother like to cook?' she asked, struggling for safer ground.

'Not if she could help it. When it was the cook's day off we ate cheese on crackers.'

Mel smothered a smile, tried to imagine crackers filling the holes in Jake's stomach.

'Don't worry,' she said. 'I'm making lots to eat.'

'But it's burned, you say?'

She could tell he was teasing by the way his eyes crinkled. Suddenly her nervousness disappeared. 'Come on,' she said, taking him by the arm. 'I'm making prawns with the steak. You can help.'

8

Jake watched Mel chase a cherry tomato around her plate. He'd been unable the whole dinner to keep his gaze off her. People said eating strawberries was the ultimate in sensuality, but he'd been entranced watching her eat prawns. The way she put them in her mouth and sucked them with ferocity, then drew out the shell end, butter dripping down her chin. He'd had to fight the inclination to lean towards her and lick up the butter with a swipe of his tongue.

'I'm full,' she said, giving up the chase with the tomato. 'But I'd love some more wine.' She held out her glass and licked her bottom lip. Desire, hot and fierce, swept through Jake again.

This dinner had been a bad idea, especially allowing her to cook it for him in her apartment. They should have gone somewhere public, somewhere it would have been easier to keep his attraction to her under wraps.

As it was he had burdened himself with a ridiculous bet when he could have finished the evening with her body next to his.

His resolve would melt, Jenny had said. Jesus, she was right.

The first thing he had to do was stop watching Mel's lips, stop imagining sucking the fingers curled around her glass. Jake blinked, and rapidly poured her some more wine. A drop or two spilled over the rim of the glass and ran down her hand. She laughed and lifted her fingers to her lips and, just as he had visualized, sucked them clean.

'I'll do the dishes,' he said, his voice coming out strangled.

'Don't bother,' Mel said. 'I'll do them in the morning.' She leaned towards him and touched his hand. 'Come on, let's go sit in the living room and relax.'

The living room was actually just the end of this room, yet despite the fact it was only ten feet away, he didn't want to move. Didn't trust himself being anywhere more comfortable. He'd told Jenny this chastity thing would be easy. How could he have been so wrong?

He'd imagined before he came that this attraction was controllable, that he'd be able with ease to keep his distance. But he'd reckoned without the woman herself, and the come-to-me look flashing from her eyes.

'Care for a brandy?' Mel asked.

'It's getting late. I better go.'

'Not yet,' she protested, tugging him to his feet.

She stood so close he could smell her hair, like the woman herself; fresh, clean, and infinitely appealing. The sort of scent a man could breathe in forever. He drew himself up. It was far too soon to be bandying words like *forever*. He didn't even know her. Not properly. If he wasn't careful he'd do something he'd regret.

Better just to kiss her and get the hell out.

She was close enough to kiss and her head was tilted up, her eyes looking luminous in the light of the candles she'd strewn everywhere.

'Dinner was delicious,' he said, trying to steer his thoughts away from her appeal.

'There's still dessert.'

All he wanted for dessert was to hold her in his arms, to feel her breasts crushed against his chest.

'I've made chocolate mousse.' Her tongue licked her lip.

He imagined it licking him, driving fire before it. 'I like chocolate mousse,' he said, determined to show control. He'd eat, converse a while, and then he would go, safe in the knowledge he hadn't succumbed. Jenny didn't know everything, even if she thought she did.

'Go on,' Mel said, pointing toward the sofa at the other end of the living room. 'Get comfortable. I'll bring the mousse out.'

There were candles lit in this part of the room also, and they sent up shadows, both romantic and mysterious. Where should he sit? If he chose the sofa, she would no doubt sit beside him, because of the two chairs, one looked as though its springs were broken and the other was a bean bag chair. Sprawled in such a contraption, he wouldn't feel in control. It was just the sort of place Mel might choose though. She'd curl up like a cat in its basket, all feline grace and feminine elegance.

With a groan, he sank onto the sofa and tried to relax. Mel had been funny and chatty throughout dinner, had made him laugh, yet at moments she had been serious too, had shown depths to her character to which her surface only alluded. He glanced at his watch. Eleven-thirty already. If he wasn't careful, he'd still be here for the witching hour.

She'd already begun to cast her spell over him. Good thing he was strong.

'You're looking awfully serious.'

He glanced up and found her

standing next to the sofa holding a tray laden with coffee and dessert. He reached up. 'Let me take that.' Their fingers touched. Shock waves shot through him, and the frown already creasing his brow burrowed deeper.

He set the tray on the coffee table. She joined him on the sofa. Her thigh touched his as she leaned forward to pour and heat sparked between them like flint striking rock.

She turned to him with a quizzical look. 'What are you thinking about?'

'You.' He pulled in a breath. If he wanted to leave without kissing this woman, giving her a compliment was not the best way. Women liked knowing men were thinking of them. In the past he'd used it often as part of the mating game. This time it was true, and was having the same effect.

Her eyes, already luminous, darkened and grew larger, and her cheeks flushed in the glow of the lit candles.

Unable to resist, he stretched out his hand. Her cheek, when he touched it, was soft and warm. Just a touch, a friendly gesture after a good meal, not something to worry about, to fear future complications.

Then his fingers moved of their own accord, touching her temple then behind on her neck, drawing her face across toward his.

The last time he'd experienced an explosion when they kissed. This time was much slower, more thorough, more intense. She sucked away his breath, yet energized his body, until every sinew and muscle seemed alive.

Just a minute more. That was all he'd allow. Just a minute to taste the inside of her mouth.

She tasted of chocolate, as though she'd licked her fingers after filling their bowls. But behind the chocolate was her own sweet taste. Then her tongue touched his and he lost all ability to analyze anything. All he knew was desire, compelling him forward.

His fingers twisted around her hair, became entangled in its silkiness. He pulled her even closer, his senses reeling. Then she fell against him, her chest pressing against his arm, and he felt at last the nipples of her breasts. Her arms entwined around his neck. When her fingers touched his ears, he felt them burn.

'You're hot,' she whispered, licking his ear as if to cool it.

He found it had entirely the opposite effect. Eastern philosophers must know of what they spoke when they said all body parts were connected to each other, for he could feel her tongue thrust its way deep inside, and places far distant from his head began to throb.

'Are you hot here?' she asked, redirecting her attention back to his temple then kissing a circuitous path to his mouth.

Without conscious thought his hands wandered to her back and slipped beneath the fabric of her silky top. Without a bra to encumber, he had full range, and his fingers caressed every inch. He could feel her spine with its bumps and ridges, could feel, also, the muscles and curves of her body.

She moaned.

Their kiss deepened.

Her mouth opened wide.

He lost all intention to end the encounter.

Then she pulled away, her gaze locked on his.

'Mel,' he said.

She swallowed, her eyes filling with desire, with something else, also . . . uncertainty . . . confusion . . . a myriad of emotions.

He bit back further words.

He wanted her. She wanted him. He had to stop. He feared he couldn't. He longed with an ache to be naked beside her, to feel her silken skin against his own. He felt her heat as though fanned by a fire.

You'll melt, Jenny had told him, and he feared she was right. You'll never make it, Jenny had added, to the end of the summer without succumbing to having sex. He had to prove his assistant wrong, had to focus past his primal urges.

'The Mariners are doing great this season,' he said.

Mel's eyes widened. 'Is that your version of talking dirty?' she asked. 'Ichiro's hot,' she added, in a throaty whisper, 'but not as hot as you.'

Jesus, why had Jenny finally been wrong? She'd sworn talking sports was a turn-off with women. Obviously, with Mel, it had the opposite effect.

He'd have to call a halt in some other way. He couldn't screw up again as he almost had with Tammy and create a baby with a woman he scarcely knew.

'I want you,' she said, trying to tug his shirt off. 'Take me,' she said, pressing against him.

He wanted to touch her, to feel her breasts, to lick her sweetness with his tongue, but he had to slow his racing breath, had to rein in his emotions. If he didn't, he'd be lost, and so would his bet.

'Make love to me,' she whispered, biting her lip, the gesture striking Jake as incredibly sensual.

He touched her cheek again. 'It's time I left.'

'You can't leave now.' Her chest felt tight, and the heat she had felt suddenly congregated on her face.

She'd tried to force an intimacy with this man. Now he wanted to leave. What had she done wrong? Did her lack of experience show? Or did he find her unattractive, inexperienced, or worse?

'I've got to go,' he said again, shifting beside her.

'You have to stay.' She had to make him finish what they'd started. 'Stay,' she cajoled, leaning forward to kiss him.

His lips were hard, didn't yield to her caress.

She pulled back, stared into his eyes.

His lids were half closed, preventing her from seeing, but his chin was thrust out as though with determination.

'I want you,' she whispered, taking a

leap into the unknown.

'I've got to go,' he said again, but more gently this time. 'It's getting late. Trish will be home soon.'

Mel felt a sudden panic. It had cost her hugely to force this encounter, but despite the way she was throwing herself at Jake, she was still a virgin. If he left, she wasn't sure she could do this again.

He stood, took a step, then stopped and gazed down at her. He looked amazing when seen from a slight distance, was hard and lean and rippled with muscles. She longed to touch him, to reconnect, to let the magnetic force between them draw them closer. Uncurling her legs, she stood also.

'Don't you want me?' she asked.

'It's not that — '

'Then what is it?' She forced all expression from her face, determined to mask the pain in her soul. 'It's just sex,' she went on, trying to sound hip. 'It's easy. No strings.'

'You won't feel that way tomorrow.'

'Let me worry about tomorrow.'

'There's more to it than that.'

This was not the way this conversation was supposed to go. From all she had heard, men wanted only one thing: unencumbered sex, given freely without regret.

So why wasn't Jake jumping at that offer? Why was he standing there stern-faced and judging?

Her first conclusion must be right. He must find her lacking.

She lifted her chin. Eight years of dreams and wide-awake fantasies hadn't even come close to matching the reality of this man. But in her dreams he'd never once rejected her, had never left her feeling as she did now.

She tugged down her blouse, wishing that it covered her better, trying not to betray how hurt she felt. 'Drink your coffee, eat your mousse. Don't feel you have to leave on my account.' She could still feel the heat where his hands had touched her, and that filled her with an anger she hadn't expected. She snatched up her shoes from beside the sofa, and with a swift movement, put them on.

'What are you doing?' he demanded.

'I'm going out.' She twitched her skirt straight, and searched the floor for her shoes.

'Out where?' he asked, his brows forming a straight line.

'Clubbing,' she said.

'At this hour? You can't.'

'I can and I will.'

'But why?' he growled.

'Because I want to party and you won't oblige.'

He stepped toward her.

She could smell him . . . touch him. She stepped away, her head spinning.

He reached out a hand. 'Don't go. You don't have to.'

For an instant she reveled in the electricity between them, then she shook off his hand and stared into his eyes. 'That's where you're wrong. Why should I stay?'

'It's late.' His frown deepened. 'It's

too late to go out.'

'Do you want sex? Real sex?'

His eyes grew dark. 'Is that all you're after?'

She shrugged, said nothing.

'You can't just go out and have sex with a stranger.'

'Watch me,' she snapped. 'People do it all the time.'

9

Not people like her. Mel stared over the railing at the top of the stairs. The space below seethed with bodies, all young and sweaty and moving to the music.

It was everywhere, the music, thudding through her ears and into her veins, injecting its rhythm as a doctor would anesthetic. She only hoped it would work, for her body ached and her chest felt as though something had been ripped out.

Not her heart, she decided fiercely, but maybe her confidence, which, she prayed, would somehow regenerate in the pit below.

Gradually her eyes adjusted to the light, to the shadows and flashes of strobe lamps gone mad.

She had thought Jake would be her first lover, had been so drugged by the magic of his touch. He'd made her feel wonderful. Now she felt a fool.

Her lips pressed tight. She needed a drink. She needed something to numb her senses.

On unaccustomed heels, she teetered down the stairs, then elbowing past dancers, crossed the dance floor to the bar.

She'd have one drink, maybe two, would kill enough time until it was safe to go home. She didn't want to return too early, didn't want Trish discovering the evening had been a bust. She especially didn't want any more tips on how easy it was to bag a man.

'What would you like?' the bartender asked.

'A Zombie,' Mel replied, 'and a shot of tequila.'

* * *

Jake had followed as swiftly as he could, had locked Mel's apartment, and reached the road in time to see her get into a taxi. He hopped into one too, didn't bother with his car, and followed her at his taxi's top speed. Now he stood on the curb and stared incredulously at the sign proclaiming *The Sultan Club*.

What the hell was she thinking coming to a place like this, especially alone, and at this time of night? He hadn't believed she had meant what she said, hadn't believed she was like the other women he had known, one who looked for a good time with no commitments.

All of which didn't let him off the hook. He had to stop her doing what she meant to do. Tony would never forgive him if he didn't. The trick was that while saving her, he had to keep his distance, had to banish from his mind how she felt in his arms. For when he remembered, his body turned hard and, at the same time, his will turned soft.

Without getting too close, he had to convince her to leave this place and go home where it was safe. Shouldn't be too hard.

He paid off the cab driver and made for the club entrance, brushed past the bouncer and surveyed the premises. He spotted her fast, already dancing, her hand clutching an already empty glass. The man she was with looked like a player, too good-looking, too smooth, too much for the inexperienced. He danced too close in a song that didn't require it; was cheek to cheek, chest to chest, and worst of all, hip to hip.

Too cool, too hot, too ready for action. The sort of fellow who would take advantage of a woman. Especially a woman as inexperienced as Mel. And Mel was inexperienced. He was sure of *that* much, despite her ability to turn him on.

Air exploded from Jake's lungs. He'd only known Mel for a few days. He shouldn't care this much, didn't know how to stop caring. He started down the steps, fists ready to swing.

She smiled when he reached her then turned her back.

'I'm cutting in,' he growled.

'I don't think so,' she said.

He grabbed her arm and swung her around.

'What do you want?' she demanded.

'Let's go,' Jake replied, glaring at her partner as he took hold of Mel's waist and pulled her once more into the dance.

'I just got here,' Mel said, 'but if you're headed to the bar, I could use another drink.'

'You've had enough already.' Her partner's hand slid down Mel's bare back. A pulse began to throb at Jake's temple. 'Watch it, buddy.' He slapped the man's hand away.

'You know this dude?' the slimeball asked Mel.

'Nope,' she replied, slanting Jake a look.

'I'm her lawyer,' he snapped, then clenching his fists, barely resisted the urge to punch the guy.

'No way,' the man said, nibbling Mel's ear. 'What did you do?'

'Nothing yet,' she replied, then

slowly, sexily, directed her lips to her partner's neck.

'Enough,' Jake growled. 'I'm taking you home.'

'Hey, man,' her partner protested, 'quit bothering the lady.'

Mel smiled smugly and pressed closer to the man's gyrating body.

Jake grabbed him by the shoulder. 'She's dancing with me.' He tossed the slimeball a crumpled twenty and jerked his head in the direction of the bar. 'Buy yourself a drink,' he ordered, 'then get lost.'

Jake turned back to Mel and took her in his arms, realizing too late he'd sworn not to get close.

'So you've changed your mind?' Mel whispered in his ear.

Her breath held the scent and intoxication of tequila. 'You're drunk,' he accused.

'I'm working on it.' Suddenly, she sagged against him.

'I'm getting you out of here,' Jake told her gruffly.

'My place or yours?' she asked, with a smile.

In his arms, she felt even better than Jake remembered. Certain sections of his body went on instant alert. It was dangerous to have gone to her rescue. If he wasn't careful, someone would have to rescue him. And there was no one on this mine field they called a dance floor who could succeed in prying her loose from his arms. Not now he was holding her.

'You haven't answered my question,' she went on, her voice low.

'Your place,' he said firmly.

'Only if you come too.' Her half closed eyes opened and focused on him then she drew nearer and kissed his lips.

The electricity the kiss created singed his feet to the floor. Before he knew what he was doing, he was kissing her back.

'That's more like it,' she said, darting her tongue across his lips. Then she pressed against him, her breasts crushed against his chest.

He palmed her back and pulled her closer. If he'd been hot for her before, now he was ablaze.

With a smile on her lips and her eyes smoldering secrets, she tilted up her head and captured his ear.

With a groan, he buried his face in her neck. She smelled the same as she had back in her apartment, and her skin was even softer than before.

She thrust her tongue into his ear. 'Come home with me.'

His brain flowed like lava to his lower regions. He struggled to keep his head clear, struggled to remember his plan. He'd come to this place to keep Mel safe, not wreak desecration on Tony's cousin himself.

Jesus, Tony's cousin. What the hell was he doing? And how could he face Jenny if he went on this way?

'Hey, boss man,' a voice suddenly said.

He knew that voice better than his own. With a groan, Jake twisted in

Mel's arms. Jenny stood before him, one hand on her hip, and her usually tied-back hair falling loose to her shoulders. 'What are you doing here?' Jake demanded.

'I'm here with Scott Baxter.' Jenny's face was flushed and her eyes were dancing, and it wasn't due to catching him in the arms of a bet-blasting siren. She grinned at him happily.

'Scott Baxter? My client?'

'The one and the same.'

'So where is he?'

'Getting me a drink.'

Jake frowned. 'You're not supposed to go out with Scott unless I lose the bet.'

'You look like you're well on your way to that now.' Jenny nodded toward Mel, who still swayed on her own, her skirt hiked high and her eyes half closed.

'This is not what it seems,' he mumbled.

She lifted one brow.

'I'm taking her home.'

'He's coming with me,' Mel said, swaying against Jake.

He held her tightly so she could maintain her balance.

'Your home or hers?' Jenny asked Jake tartly.

'Hers,' he replied, struggling to keep Mel upright. 'She's had too much to drink. I'm taking her home then leaving.'

'Not leaving,' Mel said. She closed her eyes and kissed Jake's chin.

'Just the two of you together?' Jenny's grin broadened. 'I'll be expecting my check in the morning, boss man.'

'What check?' Mel mumbled.

'Just a bet Jake and I have.'

'Bet?' Mel's eyes fluttered open then just as swiftly fluttered shut again.

Jake shot a warning in Jenny's direction.

'Ask Jake,' Jenny added hastily.

Mel loosened her grip, seemed to struggle to train her focus on him. 'Jake?' she asked.

'Jenny and I are always betting. Over

who can drink the most cups of coffee in a day, or who can string together the most paper clips — that sort of thing.'

Mel's eyes narrowed.

'We made a bet once,' Jenny went on, 'as to who could kiss the longest.'

Jake could cheerfully have wrung his assistant's neck.

'That sounds like fun,' Mel said, her voice slurred. 'Who won?'

'Jake always wins when it comes to kissing.' Jenny cast him a teasing look then turned back to Mel. 'But you probably know that by now.'

'We have kissed,' Mel said, showering them both with a wobbly smile before cuddling once again close to Jake.

'She's not herself,' Jake explained, 'and you're not helping.'

'Just trying to get the picture,' Jenny replied virtuously.

'There is no picture!'

Mel frowned. 'That's not true. There's a picture. There could have been more of a picture.' She tapped Jake on the arm. 'But Jake said he had to go home.' She turned to Jenny and shook her head. 'He's not much fun.'

Jenny laughed. 'He's just tired. He's been working too hard.'

'Jenny!' Jake warned.

'Then we have to do something about that.' Mel drew a wavy line down his chest.

Jake wished she would stop. He didn't want Jenny guessing how much Mel's touch affected him, how desperately he wanted to touch her back.

Mel hooked her fingers under his belt. 'I know,' she said. 'We'll have a party.'

Jake brushed her hand away. 'What sort of party?'

'A house party,' Mel said, 'at my family's cabin on Birch Lake. You're all invited.' She turned to Jenny. 'Bring your date.'

'I don't think — ' Jake began.

'Quite right,' Mel interrupted. 'Best not to think. We'll swim, barbeque some steaks, relax in the hot tub.'

'Maybe some other time.' The last

thing he wanted was to sit next to Mel half naked!

'We'd love to,' Jenny countered.

Jake shot her a furious look.

'That's settled then,' Mel said. 'We'll head out Saturday morning.' She dangled her empty glass from between two fingers. 'Did someone say they were getting drinks?'

'No more for you,' Jake said firmly. He took the glass from her and placed it on a table. 'You've had enough.'

'You can never have enough Zombies,' Mel protested.

'Have you ever drunk them before?'

'I'm not sure.' She giggled. 'It doesn't seem to matter.'

Jake winced at the sight of the grin on Jenny's face. 'We're going,' he said, urging Mel towards the stairs. 'I'll see you tomorrow, Jenny,' he called over his shoulder.

'Champion kisser,' Mel murmured happily, her step unsteady as she stumbled up the stairs beside him. 'Let's go back to my place and practice.'

'You're going to bed.'

'Sounds perfect,' she purred, tripping over the top step.

Jake caught her before she fell. She swayed against him and closed her eyes. 'Bed,' she said, dreamily. 'Have to go to bed. You have to come too. Have to do this tonight.'

'Do what tonight?'

'Make love.'

'Why tonight?'

'It's time. Past time,' she corrected herself.

'Past time for what?'

'For making love. Aren't you listening?'

'I'm listening.' The air was hot. It blended with the heat cocooning them both.

'I need you to make love to me.'

He frowned and gripped her waist more firmly, then led her to a cab.

'So you're a champion kisser,' she went on. Her eyes shone as though she'd been handed a prize.

When she looked at him like that,

something moved inside him. His heart seemed suddenly to beat in a different way.

'Come home with me,' she entreated.

Without answering he opened the door to his cab and lowered her inside. His hand lingered for an instant on her waist, then he climbed in beside her and she relaxed her head against his shoulder.

He could still smell her hair again and the scent of her body — all hot and musky and redolent of summer nights. He swallowed hard and gave the cab driver directions. He didn't know if it was the purr of the car's engine, or the wine with dinner topped with Zombies, but before they had gone more than a couple of blocks, Mel's breathing deepened and she closed her eyes in sleep.

As they drove through Seattle's night-black streets, Jake was aware only of her. He wanted her, needed her, was determined not to have her. When they got to her apartment, he shook her shoulder. She stirred and stretched, then snuggled closer.

The desire to kiss her overwhelmed him. Even asleep, she was just as appealing as she had been while awake. He would have to carry her in and deposit her on her bed, but once he'd done that, he'd get the hell out. Remove himself before he acted on impulse.

He paid the driver then edged himself from beneath Mel. He was sure she would stir when he put his arms around her and lifted her up and out of the car, but she linked her arms around his neck and tucked her face into his shoulder, relaxing like a child in his arms.

Only Mel was no child. Her curves and soft skin made his senses quicken.

In the taxi, he had taken her key from her purse, and he inserted it now into the downstairs lock. The door opened, they entered and he made for the elevator, smiling faintly at an old couple who cast them openly curious stares.

In the elevator, she shifted in his

arms, and still seeming to sleep, lifted her lips to his. They were warm and soft and seemed to fit his perfectly, were the kiss of a dream lover enticing him to make love.

When the elevator opened, he walked out in a daze, clinging to the little self-control he had left.

A second key, a second lock, a second twist of a handle and in too short a time they were safely in her apartment.

Alone together, the antithesis of safety.

He knew which room was hers, but as they drew near, his footsteps slowed. It was here he would have to let her go.

A stained glass lamp glowed next to her bed and her quilt was pulled down as though awaiting their return. The window was not glistening with sunlight now, but a ray of moonlight shafted through. It blazed a path from the door to Mel's bed.

In the doorway, Jake paused, his heart pounding. His throat grew dry, but he stepped over the threshold and prepared to face the demons inside: desire, temptation, lust and need. All powerful forces in the renouncement of love.

All facing him with this woman on this night.

He tightened his jaw and moved toward her bed, where he laid her down and gently disengaged his hand.

She curled onto her side and sighed out a sweet breath, the sound seeming to whisper his name. His groin tightened, his chest expanded, heat flushed through his system, and slowly, gently, he touched her face.

With a moan, she turned and pressed her face to his palm. Then, half asleep, she lifted an arm and took hold of his hand. She held it a minute before raising it for a kiss.

'Jake,' she whispered, her breath fluttering his fingers.

He caught in a breath then replied softly, 'Mel.'

His voice seemed to sooth her. Her lips formed a smile. She tugged on his hand, pulling him onto the bed beside her. He raised her in his arms and captured her to him, not caring suddenly about silly bets.

His lips met Mel's in an explosion of heat, and if she was a dream lover, she certainly felt real.

'Make love to me,' she begged.

There was no question of quenching the fire between them this time with talk of baseball and first-year players.

'You'll be my first,' she added, opening her eyes, and staring up at him with trust and vulnerability.

'Your first?' he exclaimed. Could that be true? A woman like her, so exciting, so beautiful, must have made love to a man before.

Although Tony had always said his family was old-fashioned, and made that statement with centuries-old Italian pride.

Despite the odds against it, Mel could be a virgin. Which made it even more vital for him to leave. This evening he had protected her from other men. Now he had to protect her from himself.

'I'm going home,' he said gruffly.

In response, she rubbed against him like a cat.

'Go to sleep,' he ordered.

'Saturday,' she said, speaking the word clearly.

'What about it?' he asked.

'We'll make love then.' She smiled at him suddenly, a radiant smile, then as his heart warmed, she closed her eyes.

He opened his mouth, intending to protest, then shut it again without uttering a word. Mel was in no condition for conversation. With luck she wouldn't remember anything she'd just said, or would be too embarrassed to bring it up again. And if by chance she did, he'd simply come up with an excuse not to go to her family's cabin and spend the day fending off advances he longed to accept.

10

'What time are we leaving?' Jenny asked.

'Leaving for where?' Jake frowned at the papers littering his desk. He'd been working on Jessie Parker's file for the last hour, fighting the knowledge he needed to talk to the elderly woman. But if he went to her house, he'd probably see Mel.

He hadn't seen Mel or talked to her since the previous Saturday night, but he hadn't been able to banish her from his mind. And every time she entered it, he needed a cold shower.

'Mel's cabin,' Jenny said impatiently. 'Where we're going this weekend.'

'I haven't heard from Mel. I doubt she remembers asking us, and if she does, she's probably called the whole thing off.'

'Nice try,' Jenny said. She waited

until he signed the top paper then lifted it away, revealing the next. 'Nothing's been called off,' Jenny went on, 'and nothing's going to stop me from spending the weekend with Scott.'

Jake looked up. 'Scott? Are you really taking him? What will Sam say if you go off for a weekend with some guy?'

'Sam's staying with my parents and is looking forward to being spoiled rotten. And for your information he adores Scott. Ever since he came to watch Sam play baseball.'

'Be careful, Jenny,' Jake said worriedly. 'You don't want things to move too fast.'

Jenny laughed. 'That's usually my line.' Then her face grew serious. 'You haven't said anything about the other night. Let's have it. What happened? Did you and Mel have sex?'

'No,' he replied sharply. 'When I make a promise, I keep it.'

'Just checking,' Jenny grinned. 'I can always ask Mel.'

He glared at her. 'You wouldn't dare!

Besides, you barely know her.'

'We've talked,' Jenny said.

'When?'

'She called here this morning.'

'This morning? What did she want?' He felt his face grow hot. 'Why didn't you put her through to me?'

'She wasn't calling to talk to you.'

'So what did she want?'

'Just wanted to give me directions to her cottage.'

So Mel hadn't discarded the cozy weekend idea. She had a disconcerting way of making him guess wrong. He didn't like it. Damn.

'She didn't want to disturb you,' Jenny went on, 'said she knew you were busy. She also said you could pick her up at ten o'clock Saturday morning.'

'I'm not going,' he said.

Jenny placed her hands on her hips and stared at him sternly. 'You have to go. If you don't, Mel will call the whole thing off and any hopes I have of getting to know Scott better will go down the tubes.'

'There's nothing stopping you and Scott from getting together without us.'

Jenny's eyes narrowed. 'You're chicken,' she accused.

'I'm not chicken.'

'You're afraid of Mel, afraid you'll succumb to her charms if you spend time with her.'

'I'm not afraid of any woman.'

'Then prove it,' Jenny demanded. 'Come on this weekend and show me you can resist.'

'Nothing easier.' Yet his body still ached from trying to resist. Perhaps he was making too much of this. Perhaps it had only been difficult the other night because he'd felt protective of Mel. At her own cottage there would be no need to act the hero, no reason to be closer to her than Jenny or Scott.

Besides which, he told himself reassuringly, there was always safety in numbers.

★ ★ ★

Why the hell hadn't Jenny and Scott accepted a lift? If they'd been here, he wouldn't be alone with Mel. He glanced to his right, caught her staring eagerly out the window, as though waiting to catch the first glimpse of familiar landmarks.

'There!' She turned towards him, her face alight, as she pointed to a log house resting on a wide point of land jutting into the lake.

Jake estimated the length and width of the house. 'That's no cottage.' It was big enough to have at least four bedrooms. From the distance, he could also see a log cabin out the back, mirroring the main house in everything but size.

'That's where you'll sleep,' Mel said, following his gaze. 'It's very cozy . . . private.'

He didn't want private. If he was to get through this weekend without faltering on his vow, he would have to make sure they all hung out together. He'd told Jenny he'd have no problem resisting Mel's attractions, but sitting next to her now, he knew that wasn't true.

Everything about her attracted him: her hair, her long legs, the smell of her perfume. With an oath, he yarded the steering wheel sharply left and entered the long drive leading to the house.

Thank God, Jenny and Scott were already there, sitting comfortably on wooden chairs on the wrap-around porch. One glance at Jenny's face filled him with concern, for it was not the face of a woman craving group activities, but rather of a woman looking to be alone with a man. Jenny's face was flushed and her lips tilted upward at every word Scott uttered.

Jake felt happy for his friend, but without Jenny's help it would be tough to keep his feelings for Mel at bay. With a sigh, he turned the key and cut the car's engine.

Mel sank back against her seat, seemed to drink in the lack of sound.

'It's always so quiet here,' she murmured contentedly.

'Too quiet,' Jake muttered. Already he could feel the peace seep in through his pores and relax the guard he'd been erecting against Mel.

But he couldn't falter now he knew she'd never been with a man. He could only hope Mel would think things through and realize that what she really wanted was the sort of relationship he was seeking. One built on intimate knowledge of each other's hearts and souls, not the shallow physicality of mindless sex.

He only wished mindless sex wasn't so hard to give up.

'Jake,' Mel said again.

He spun around to face her.

Mel touched his arm. 'You were a million miles away.' She suddenly longed to kiss him, as she'd done last Saturday on the way home from the club.

Thanks to the Zombies, she didn't remember much about that night, but

199

one thing stood out crystal clear in her mind; she'd asked and he'd promised to make love to her. Only properly this time, putting an end to her virginity.

She drew her hand down his arm, curled her fingers around his. 'Let's unload the car,' she suggested, 'then go sit in the hot tub.'

'A brisk walk would be better.' He glanced in the direction of Jenny and Scott. 'We can all go together.'

'I was thinking just the two of us.' She squeezed his fingers. 'I'm sure Jenny and Scott want some time alone too.'

A frown furrowed Jake's brow. 'Look, Mel, about what you said. It's not a good idea.'

'Why?' she asked, withdrawing her hand.

Jake's eyes darkened. 'Making love is a serious thing.'

'Not according to my friend Trish.'

'It's not something to embark on lightly.'

She chuckled. 'My family says I never

do anything lightly.'

'But why this? Why with me?'

'I already told you why.' She turned away, couldn't look at him.

'You said that you've never made love before.'

The gentleness in his voice denoted pity, and if she met his gaze, she was sure she would see it in his eyes also. She faced the water instead, willing her beating heart to slow its rhythm to that of the soft waves lapping the shore.

'It's not because no one has ever wanted to,' she said tightly.

'I'm sure it isn't,' he replied.

Reluctantly, she faced him.

'You're beautiful,' he went on. 'I'm not sure you know how much. You shouldn't rush something like this.'

'Being twenty-four and still a virgin is not rushing anything.'

'You should take your time.' He captured her hand. 'Enjoy the experience.'

'I intend to enjoy it.'

'Then why do you look so grim?'

She took a deep breath and tried to relax, tried to affect an air of fun and sophistication. 'I'm not grim.' She forced a smile to her lips. 'I'm simply tired of waiting. Having sex is no big deal.' She leaned towards him and kissed his shoulder.

He cast a sharp glance in Jenny and Scott's direction. 'Believe me,' he said, 'it can be a very big deal.'

'What do you mean?'

'What if you get pregnant?'

She smiled. 'That doesn't need to happen in this day and age.'

'Sometimes it does.'

'Not if you're careful,' she protested.

'When you're having a good time, you're not always careful.'

She stared into his eyes, knew that what he said was true. Making love with Jake would empty all thought, would leave no room for plans and control. Which simply meant she'd have to plan ahead.

For Jake was right about one thing. She didn't want to get pregnant and jeopardize all she'd worked for, to throw away her studies before they even began. To say nothing of the fact she didn't want a baby.

Not now, maybe not ever. There was no time for children if she intended to be a surgeon. 'I don't want to talk about this now,' she said to Jake.

'You're right.' He sighed. 'Jenny and Scott are waiting. They're probably wondering why we've been sitting here so long.'

Mel glanced toward the porch. 'They don't look as though they're missing us at all.' Jake's assistant and her friend were talking to each other as though they couldn't talk fast enough. And their fingers were interlocked like rose vines over an arbor.

Mel forced away the jealousy pricking her heart. She didn't want what Jenny might be building with Scott. All she wanted was sex, and she wanted it soon.

'We'll talk later,' Jake said.

'I don't care if we never talk.' Once

again, she closed her fingers around Jake's, felt a shiver of anticipation when she did so. 'Talking's overrated.'

* * *

Jake flung his case to the foot of his bed and cursed himself as every sort of a fool. He'd underestimated Mel, had overestimated himself, had thought he was too experienced to be sucked in by a woman with black hair and green eyes.

What had happened to his control, to his ability to weigh and evaluate, to determine the best path and follow it no matter what?

A week ago, he'd been a man who would jump at the chance of sex. Now when he wanted more, the woman he was with didn't.

He unzipped his bag. Maybe Mel didn't know what she wanted. Maybe she was trying to play it cool to make a man interested.

If he told her what he wanted, maybe she would change.

Jake pulled some shorts from his bag and hastily flung them on. He would take her for a walk. Talk to her. Change her.

★ ★ ★

When she looked as she did now, he didn't want to change a thing. She sat on the porch railing swinging her legs, laughing at something Jenny or Scott said, behaving as if she'd known them her entire life.

She looked up when he opened the glass-paneled French doors, and smiled just for him, a heart-stopping smile. It extended to her eyes and to her body too, so that it seemed he would drown in the warmth of her welcome. It was not the face of a woman solely interested in sex.

The women with whom he'd had affairs in the past had flirted in a totally different manner than this. They'd beckoned with their bodies but never with their souls, while Mel, in contrast, managed to do both.

When he reached her, she stood and faced him, her body leaning towards his, as though it was natural to fall into his arms. Instinctively, he held out his hand. Instead of taking hold, she placed her hand on his elbow. The minute she touched him, he wanted more.

Mel's eyes darkened and took on a jeweled brilliance, but even the warmth in her expression didn't match that of her body. If he took another step, she would be in his arms and her full red lips would land on his.

'For goodness sake,' Jenny said, her voice reaching his ear muffled as though it was coming through a fog, 'just kiss the woman.'

One kiss couldn't hurt, not here on Mel's front porch with Jenny and Scott watching. A swift peck on the cheek. A mere brushing of lips. He leaned towards her.

She looked up.

He caught her lips. Felt immediately as though he'd come home.

'Mmm,' Mel said softly, breaking their connection. 'Jenny is right. Your kisses are world class.'

He felt dazed, disoriented. He shook his head to clear it. This wasn't going as he planned. He wanted Mel to think like him, not entice him to give in to her needs.

Jenny chuckled. 'You two look as though you've done that before.'

Jake glanced at his assistant, saw the question in her eyes. 'Once or twice,' he said. 'No harm in a little kiss.' Then, hoping to divert, he asked, 'What about you two?'

Jenny laughed and squeezed Scott's hand. 'None of your business, boss.'

Jake looked at Scott through narrowed eyes. He'd better be as good a guy as he seemed. Jenny deserved nothing but the best.

Scott put his arm around Jenny's shoulders. 'Jenny and I thought we'd go out on the lake. You two want to come?'

'We're going for a walk,' Mel replied swiftly.

Jenny cast Mel a look of approval.

Jake caught the glance and frowned. Surely, Mel wouldn't have confided in Jenny, told her she wanted to have sex with him. If she had, Jenny would think the bet was as good as won.

Jake's frown deepened. The bet itself was no longer really important, but the purpose behind the bet was more important than ever. He wanted to make love to Mel, but more than that, he wanted to get to know her.

* * *

'They're a long way out,' Jake said worriedly. He gazed through the trees lining the shore, to where Jenny and Scott sat in a motionless boat. 'Why aren't they moving?'

Mel glanced toward the water. 'They're talking,' she said.

Which was exactly what he and Mel should be restricting themselves to. But with the sunlight dappling through the trees, creating pools of gold on Mel's dark hair, more insistent than talking came the urge to touch her, to push her hair back and find the light in her eyes. He bent down, almost kissed her, found her staring back at him. Uncertainty tinged with desire lurked in her eyes, along with a curious vulnerability in one so determined.

'Kiss me,' Mel said hoarsely.

He smiled and touched her lips, knew immediately he could lose himself in their taste and texture.

They'd been walking along the spit of land on which the house was built, through a stand of trees toward the road. But the swish of occasional cars sounded far away, and seemed a hushed backdrop to the magic of the place.

'Kiss you here?' Jake asked, dropping a kiss on her cheek.

'Here,' Mel answered, offering him her lips.

She moaned when instead he shifted lower to her neck, just where her flesh emerged from her sleeveless top. 'That works too,' Mel said, with a sigh.

'I swore I wouldn't do this,' he said hoarsely.

'Why not?' She touched his face. 'You know you want to.'

'I can't deny that. But the whole purpose of this walk was to talk.'

'My friend says men don't like to talk.' At least not when they had a willing woman at their side. That was the bliss and the agony of the species. You never knew where you stood, just that the journey was incredible.

'Your friend's got it wrong,' Jake said sharply.

'Oh yeah? You want to discuss politics or sports?'

He grinned and touched her hair with his hand.

Luckily she didn't need to hear anything he had to say. All she needed was his body. She couldn't allow other considerations to impede her focus, or create a future that included someone else.

She had worked too hard, wanted too much, couldn't afford to give it up for the love of a man.

She pulled away, stunned that the word love had entered her head. All she wanted was a quick exchange of bodily fluids and the experience of intimacy with another human being.

Lab work, that was all.

'Let's go back.' She needed time to think. 'It'll be better at the cabin, more privacy . . . more comfort.' She glanced around the clearing, thought it looked like magic. But magic wasn't what she wanted. Magic had connotations of being in love.

'We'll have a hot tub,' she suggested again, not wanting to think of love.

'Sounds good,' Jake said. 'I'd like to get to know you better.'

Getting to know him wasn't in her plan. Make love, then leave, was what was best. No fuss, no mess, no emotional entanglements. 'I know everything I need to know,' she said.

'You don't know the half of it,' he promised.

11

Where the hell was Jenny? Whenever he didn't want her, she was always around. Now when he could use her she was nowhere to be seen. Jake sank lower into the hot tub until the water covered his head. It was hot, but he stayed under as long as he could bear it.

He'd never before used one woman to protect him from another, but he needed to do that now, before he gave in to temptation and made love to Mel.

He blew some water out of his mouth. He didn't actually want Jenny to know anything about him and Mel, for his relationship with Mel had gone far beyond a bet. Had become something personal . . . intimate . . . special.

Another reason he had to stay true to his vow. A stupid bet he'd made with Jenny didn't matter in the long run, but he wanted this thing between Mel and him to grow, to turn into the sort of relationship he craved.

'There you are,' a voice said softly.

He turned to see Mel emerge from the house, a batik sarong knotted around her neck. Jake's pulse quickened. It was impossible to tell what she wore underneath.

'I was beginning to think you weren't coming,' he said.

She flushed, stood before him, hesitated a moment, then with a swift movement, untied her sarong.

He'd expected a bikini, all strings and wisps of fabric, but the black one-piece Mel wore was even sexier than that. It accentuated her curves and feminine body and layered her breasts with a webbing of black lace.

'Are you naked?' she asked, peering down at the frothing water coursing over and under him.

'Come in and find out.' His words made him want to hit his head with his hand. Why the hell hadn't he told her he was clothed to his knees? Whenever he wasn't with her, he swore to stop this flirtation, then when they got together his natural instincts took over, instincts which had dropped him into trouble before this.

The sort of trouble he never wanted again. Not until he was with a woman he could love. A woman like Mel.

She sucked on her lower lip and slowly entered the tub, the water bubbling between her legs as she walked down the steps.

'Any sign of Jenny and Scott yet?' she asked.

'Nope.' He watched the water wet her suit around her breasts, puckering her nipples into tight nubs. She sat down opposite, didn't come close at all. But she was near enough for her feet to touch his.

The minute they touched, his feet tingled as though she'd taken a feather to them and his gut tingled too as need coursed through it.

'Come sit next to me,' he suggested. Mel's eyes danced. 'I thought you wanted to talk.' A drop of flung-up water sparkled on her black lashes.

'We do need to clarify some things,' he agreed.

'What sort of things?' Her breasts glistened from the top of her swimsuit as she leaned toward him.

'Like what the hell it is you want?' He fought the urge to pull her to him, fought the frustration building inside.

'I don't want anything.'

'You want to have sex.'

She shrugged. 'Not too difficult, I presume?'

'What about love?'

'I'm not looking for love.'

He frowned. 'Most women are.'

'I'm not most women.'

'What about commitment?' he demanded.

'That's the last thing I want.'

Jake rolled his shoulders, tried to throw off the tension. 'What about children?' he asked more softly.

'What about them?' She lifted water in her hands and splashed it on her breasts. It ran in rivulets down her pearly flesh, disappearing at last between her cleavage.

He averted his gaze from her breasts, was caught by her eyes instead. 'You must want them,' he said.

'No,' she replied.

'All women want children.' He wanted them too. Before the crisis with Tammy he hadn't realized just how much.

'You have a lot of opinions as to what women want.'

'The propagation of the species is instinctual they say.'

She grinned. 'What's instinctual is to have sex.'

'Sex can lead to babies.'

Mel gazed into Jake's eyes, reached forward and touched his hand. 'I don't want to talk about babies.' A throbbing began just below her left temple. It was time he stopped talking and do what men did — act on impulse, not think about consequences.

Then his jaw line tightened and his eyes grew darker. She wanted to reassure him, to tell him not to worry, but that was impossible for she was worrying too. Nothing seemed as simple as Trish had said.

'If you're planning,' Jake growled, 'on having sex, you'd better start thinking about the possibility of babies.'

'I don't plan on having any accidents,' Mel replied coolly.

'Accidents are not usually something you plan.'

'But babies should be, especially in this day and age.'

'You two planning on having a baby?' came a voice.

Mel and Jake turned together in time to see Jenny exiting the house through the kitchen door. Her face was flushed, but whether from the sun or from what she'd overheard, Mel didn't know.

'Where did you come from?' Jake demanded.

'Couldn't stay on the lake forever.' She glanced at Mel then shifted her gaze to Jake. 'We thought we'd give you two some space, but we didn't think you'd be planning babies.'

'We're not planning babies.' Mel's throat tightened. 'We're just talking in general terms.'

'So you've told her then?' Jenny said to Jake.

'Told me what?' Mel demanded.

'Where's Scott?' Jake asked, ignoring Mel's question.

'Getting changed into swim trunks.' Jenny shot them a swift smile. 'Think I'll go see what's keeping him.'

As soon as she was gone, Mel faced Jake again. 'What was she talking about?'

He shrugged, didn't answer.

'Is babies what you want?'

Jake's expression grew grim. 'Yes,' he said, 'that's exactly what I want.'

*   *   *

Mel kicked at her blankets, tried to get them off her body. She couldn't breathe, couldn't think, was thinking too much, of all the things she didn't want, hadn't planned on or needed.

It should have been simple, a straightforward wham bam, an act giving her entrance to the ranks of the sexually initiated. What on earth was she doing wrong?

She sucked some air deep into her belly, held it for a moment then released it again slowly. In her first year of university, she'd attended yoga classes with Trish, had learned belly breaths worked to bring body and mind to peace. They weren't working for her now.

Nothing was working.

Uncle Paulo's remedy for problems wasn't good either. Despite the wine she'd drunk to loosen her up on the evening of her dinner date with Jake, she still hadn't managed to get him to her bed. While she'd been in an alcohol haze, Jake had remained in firm control.

Probably just as well if what he wanted was babies.

She didn't want to start imagining

the sort of baby Jake would father, but she couldn't keep the images from rolling through her mind. It would be adorable, smart, funny and strong.

She blinked her eyes and tried to banish the picture of Jake sitting on the porch with a baby on his lap. She couldn't have a child with him, didn't want one with anyone. If she wanted to be a doctor, a surgeon especially, she had to remain entanglement free; no husband, no children, no commitment of any kind. Nothing to distract her from her work.

With an explosive gust, she expelled the air trapped in her belly. All she wanted was sex, and she wanted it with Jake. She'd wanted it from the first moment she had first laid eyes on him. She was beginning to despair of ever convincing him that this was something he wanted too.

A tap sounded at her door.

She sat bolt upright. Was it Jake coming for her? She kicked off her blankets, swung her legs over the bed's side, searched for her slippers with a wiggle of her toes.

Then she caught sight of herself in her dresser mirror and hurried to the top drawer of her chest of drawers. A swift movement had it open, and she reached inside, then stripped her flannel nightie from her body and pulled on the silk negligee Trish had given her on her last birthday. A negligee she had yet to wear.

Then she swept back her hair, straightened her shoulders, and with a few steps, opened the door.

'Jenny!' she stammered.

'Were you asleep?' Jake's friend asked.

'Not yet,' she replied. 'I thought everyone else was though. Is something the matter?'

Jenny glanced down the hall toward the bedroom Mel had given her then looked even further toward Scott's room. 'I could use some advice,' she finally answered.

'What sort of advice?' Mel's lips

twisted. 'I don't exactly feel as though I know anything about anything.' She led Jenny into her bedroom, and silently gestured her into the wicker chair next to the window. She sat down on the edge of her bed.

'I don't know why I knocked on your door,' Jenny said apologetically, perching on the edge of her chair. 'I usually talk this sort of thing over with Jake.'

'Jake's in the cabin out back,' Mel broke in. 'I could go get him if you want.'

'No,' Jenny said swiftly. 'I'd . . . I'd rather talk to you. Another woman, you know.' Her shoulders suddenly slumped. 'I don't know why I'm being so stupid about this.'

'About what?' Mel asked.

'Scott,' Jenny answered, biting her lip. 'I like him.'

'Isn't that good?'

'Very,' Jenny replied. 'Which is why I want to do things right.'

'What do you mean?'

'We haven't slept together yet.'

And here she had been thinking that everyone was doing it. 'Do you want to?' Mel asked gently.

'Maybe. I think so. I'm not sure.' She sighed. 'I just don't want him to think I'm easy.'

Mel twisted her lips. 'I didn't think people thought in those terms anymore.' At least people who weren't her father and his friends.

'Trust me, they do. Especially when you've got a child and no husband in sight.' Jenny's brows met in a frown. 'Scott knows all about Sam and that he was born when I was still in high school. But I don't want Scott thinking I go to bed with every man I meet.'

'He won't think that.'

'He might.' Jenny sighed. 'Every man I've dated, and there haven't been many, either thinks I'm desperate for sex or that I'm looking for a father for my son.' Her face took on a fierce look. 'My son doesn't need a father. We're doing all right. And I wouldn't marry a man I didn't love just to give him one.'

'Have you told Scott that?'

'No.'

'Why not?'

'I don't want him to think I'm serious, because I'm not. And I doubt that he is either.'

Mel stifled a smile. 'You're thinking too much.' Trish would have been proud to hear her say that. 'Do what feels right. Chances are Scott will want what you want too.'

'Go for it you mean?'

'Absolutely. If that's what you want.' Mel couldn't believe how easy that was to say, especially when it involved people other than her and Jake.

'Are you and Jake going to go for it too?'

'Jake doesn't seem too keen.'

'He's keen,' Jenny assured her.

'Every time we get close, he pulls away.'

'Trust me, he likes you.'

'How can you tell?'

'From the way he looks at you.' Jenny grinned. 'Jake loves women, has had plenty of girlfriends, but I've never seen him look at any woman the way he looks at you.'

'Then why doesn't he want to make love to me?'

'Have you asked him?' Jenny asked.

'Not exactly.'

'Do it,' Jake's friend ordered.

'Maybe I will.'

Jenny got to her feet. 'Well, I better get going and figure out what I want to do.' She smiled and gave Mel a swift hug. 'Thanks,' she said.

Mel watched Jenny walk down the hall, and decided it was time to take action, too. If she was going to get together with Jake, it was obvious she'd have to go to him.

She would tell him what she wanted, make him see sense, would do it quickly before she lost her nerve.

She was suddenly glad she had put Jake in the guest cabin. No one would hear them out in the back. If he said no, and she was humiliated, no one would witness that, and if they made love, they could make all the sound they wanted.

Her cheeks flushed at the thought. With a swift step, she moved through the moonlit kitchen and opened the doors to the patio beyond. She kept her gaze from the direction of the hot tub and lake, kept her attention focused on Jake's cabin door.

When she got there she paused, suddenly unsure. Her heart seemed to be beating too hard to be healthy and she couldn't force her hand to open the door.

Nothing ventured, nothing gained, her grandmother had always said, although she always added, have a backup plan. Old-school Italians always had a backup plan.

She didn't want a plan. She only wanted Jake.

She turned the handle, was not surprised when the door opened as she pushed.

Jake's room was dark, but moonlight poured in through his open window revealing bunched blankets and a pillow on the floor. Obviously he had been as restless as her. With any luck, it was due to the same reason.

Silently, she crossed Jake's threshold, made her way towards the bed.

'Jake,' she whispered, touching the blankets, was stunned to find no body beneath.

'What,' he growled, 'are you doing here?'

She whirled around, saw Jake's silhouette detach from the shadows next to the window. He was naked except for a pair of boxers, and the moonlight accentuated the muscles on his chest.

Mel's belly contracted. She felt suddenly sick. She wanted Jake so much, her whole body ached.

'I've come to talk.' Her statement suddenly seemed such a lie. They'd been doing nothing but talk since he'd come back into her life. And talking was not the purpose of a no-strings-attached relationship.

She took a step forward, stopped

when she saw his face. It was hard and angular, and the expression in his eyes was forbidding and black.

He crossed his arms over his chest.

'I didn't really want to talk,' she confessed.

'What then?' he asked.

'I want to finish what we started the other night.'

'Make love, you mean?'

'Yes,' she said, lifting her chin.

'You're a virgin,' he said.

'Is that a problem?' She steeled herself for his answer. Jake would probably want someone who could match his experience, who would know how to give pleasure and take pleasure in return.

He shrugged, didn't commit.

She took a step closer, ran her hand down his chest. Her heart was thumping so hard she was sure he could hear it. 'I know what to do,' she promised.

'How to turn me on, you mean?'

'Yes.' She was trembling. Go for it, Trish had said, and she, too, had said the same thing to Jenny. Why was it so hard to put theory into practice?

'Just what would you do?' Jake asked softly.

Had he grown suddenly larger or was that her imagination?

She pushed back her shoulders, stood as straight as she could. 'What would you like me to do?' she asked.

'Take off your negligee,' he answered.

She peered at his eyes, but the shadows in the room hid his expression from view. 'Are you laughing?' she asked, suddenly suspicious.

'Why would I laugh?'

Because she couldn't believe that finally he was willing to do as she wanted. She gazed at his lips, was enticed, drawn in. As she'd been since the very first moment she'd met him.

'What would we do if I took my negligee off?' she teased.

'What would you want me to do?'

She swallowed hard, thought of all the places she'd been imagining his mouth. 'You like breasts,' she finally said. 'How would you like them trickled with honey? You could lick them until you'd sucked the sweetness off.'

'I imagine they're already sweeter than honey,' Jake said hoarsely.

Her nipples hardened and pressed against her silk negligee. 'You would take ages doing it,' she whispered, 'because that's how we'd both like it.'

'Would you beg me for more?'

'I wouldn't have to,' she promised.

He gave a low chuckle, loomed closer than ever.

'Then you'd continue down my belly, hit all the erogenous zones.'

'Do you know where they are?'

'I know you'll find them.' A tingling began that spread through her with speed. Jake didn't have to touch her to turn her on. Simply imagining what he would do appeared to be enough.

'And then?' he asked.

'You'd go lower.'

He glanced down, his gaze burning.

'You'd take your time,' she said, her voice cracking. She could feel her juices flowing, could feel the moisture between her legs. She swallowed hard. 'We've talked enough.' Every hair on her body seemed to be standing on end, waiting for the electricity of connection.

He moved closer, nearly touched her. Then he dropped his hand. 'You're a virgin,' he said softly.

Disappointment hissed out with the air from her lungs. 'We established that already.'

'If we make love I don't want you to regret it.'

'Make me not regret it.' She pressed towards him, brushed his lips with hers.

He drew away. 'I won't do it.'

'Why?' she demanded. 'If I'm not worried, why are you?'

'I want more than sex.'

'You want babies,' she said baldly.

'And what about you? What about your parents?'

'What about them?' she asked.

'What would they say?'

'Why would they say anything?'

231

'They might have an opinion about their daughter making love.'

'No one consults their parents on something like that. Besides, my mother is dead.'

Jake reached out a hand and touched Mel's shoulder. 'I'm sorry,' he said softly.

'It was a long time ago.'

He held out his arms.

She looked into his eyes. Then, with a sigh, she fell against him.

12

He made her feel so good.

She lifted her arms and wound them around his neck, pulling him close so as to kiss him back. It was as though he was honey and she was a bee. She darted, lingered, then pulled free, but never, ever let his lips grow cold.

They were hard, then soft, then hard once more. They explored her mouth, his tongue meeting hers. He tasted of everything good in this world, of wine, of mint, of clear night air. Sensations danced and freed her desire. She gasped, took in air, returned to him again.

He curled his fingers through her hair and pulled her close. There was no time for gentleness, no need for finesse. All that she wanted was his mouth on hers.

He kissed her until she forgot to breathe then found that they did their breathing together. In, out, in, out, the air came and went, but the desire she felt spiraled only upwards. She pressed against him, felt his desire too.

His lips left her mouth and explored her face, kissing her temple and the cleft of her chin. He ranged along her neck to the top of her negligee, then, with a groan, pressed his lips to her breasts. Despite the silk between them, her nipples throbbed with need, and a moan sprung up from deep within her throat.

He pulled down the straps of her negligee and wrenched the garment free of her body. It hung between them below her waist, his hips locking it in place.

He backed toward the bed, pulling her with him. The moonlight splashed his face, revealed his desire. Joy swept through her, spiraling into ecstasy. She was thrilled beyond words to make love to this man.

Not love, she amended, squelching the insistence of her heart. She couldn't afford to make love. This was simply sex. After which they would go their separate ways; she with her memories and knowledge it would bring, and he . . . what would Jake have?

A good time, she hoped, then all thoughts scattered as a wave built within, releasing moisture and pulsating sensations. Mel's negligee fell at her feet in a silken pool.

'You're beautiful,' Jake said, his eyes dark and intense, as his gaze coursed every inch of her naked body.

She felt no self-consciousness, felt only pride, for that's what she saw reflected in Jake's eyes.

He reached towards her, but didn't touch, simply ran his hands down an inch from her body. She longed to take his hands and guide them to touch her, for with each passing moment her own need grew greater. His slow hands and hot appraisal brought her closer to conflagration, and every moment they spent not entwined with each other made her desire grow deeper and stronger.

She strained towards him, but he held her off, touching her only with his hands. Then, at last, with a groan, he pulled her against him, fitting her to his body like a second layer of skin.

Trish had said that sex was wonderful, but no words could describe how incredible it felt to be experiencing it with Jake. She felt possessed by the spirit, soul and body of the man above her — her light, her love.

When she cried out, he called also, met her voice in a triumph of sound. She struggled to breathe, had difficulty doing it, had to grab mouthfuls of air to survive.

Light blinded Mel's eyes although they were shut, and her body felt drowned in a sea of sensation. The sun shone, the stars sparkled, songs played and cymbals crashed, and lying against her was the creator of these miracles. She felt peace in his arms, matched only by joy, and a deep, fulfilled contentment permeated her being.

Her arms tightened as she held him. She wasn't sure if she could ever let him go. Love, blinding and fierce, shot through her body and penetrated to the deepest recess of her soul.

This wasn't supposed to happen, not here, not now, not with this man she couldn't afford to love.

'Wow,' he whispered into her ear. 'I thought you said you were a rookie at this?'

She swallowed hard, not sure she could even speak. 'Beginner's luck,' she finally answered.

He chuckled and held her tight. 'It was luck, all right, that brought you to me.'

'It was Jessie,' she corrected.

'I might have to waive her fee.' He dropped a kiss on the end of Mel's nose.

She felt happier than she ever had in her life. Why then did she feel as though her world was spinning?

She'd wanted sex and what she got was more. She hadn't asked for love, but that's what she'd received. She gazed into Jake's eyes, felt her chest expand. Just for tonight, she would ignore her plans, would allow herself the luxury of lying in Jake's arms. Would make love to him again without fear of loving.

'Come here,' she said softly, and pulled him close.

* * *

Her back felt hot but her front felt cold. Mel twisted toward the heat, felt warm hands around her waist. Her pulse quickened as she remembered what had occurred throughout the night, the giving and taking of sensual pleasure.

'Morning,' she murmured.

In answer, he kissed her. His lips were warm and soft, but swiftly hardened, ranging over hers, breathing her air for her. Or maybe it was that she was breathing for him.

She'd thought she now knew what making love was about, but within seconds he brought her over the moon. Her skin felt like slippery silk on his satin as she cried out again, the sound this time blocking the chirping of swallows nesting in the rafters of the cabin. No moonlight now lit Jake's face into shadow, but sunlight lay bright across eyes glowing with passion.

She stared down and saw his eyes widen, saw within their light his pleasure and joy. Finally, slowly, they ceased their rocking, and she lay on his chest, dripping with sweat.

She smiled down at him. 'They say this is good exercise.'

'Beats the hell out of running,' he answered, with a smile.

She never wanted to leave this room, or the man lying beneath her. She wanted to stay here always, making love with Jake.

Making love.

Two words she couldn't even afford to think, for with a sudden rush of fear, she knew that's what they'd done. Trying not to let loose her inner panic, she pushed herself up and off of Jake.

'Where are you going?' he asked, stroking her arm.

'It's getting late. I've got to go.'

He glanced at the table beside his bed and peered at the clock sitting on it. 'It's only six o'clock.'

She swallowed hard.

He propped onto his elbow and gazed into her eyes. 'What's the matter?' he asked softly.

She couldn't answer, couldn't admit how she felt, couldn't say she would die if she couldn't love him again.

'We made love,' she said instead, her voice stumbling over the last word.

'Yes,' he answered. A shadow flitted across his face. 'Do you regret that?' he asked.

'No.' Her heart thumped. Her only regret was how she felt now. 'What about you?'

'Never.'

'You didn't want to make love before.'

'No,' he agreed.

'Why not?'

'Does it matter?'

'You said it was because I was a virgin.'

'That's right,' he murmured.

'That's not the real reason.'

His gaze shifted from hers. 'What else could there be?'

'I don't know.' She frowned. 'But Jenny implied there was something else.'

His gaze snapped back, focused on her face. 'Jenny should mind her own business.'

'Tell me,' she insisted.

'It's nothing important.'

'Then why not just say?' Whatever he was keeping from her, she needed him to say it, in order to eliminate the love she now felt and enable her to rise and leave his bed.

'It was just a bet,' he mumbled.

'A bet? What sort of bet?'

'About sex,' he admitted, his lips twisting to a grimace.

She stared at him, stunned. How

could he have bet he could make her sleep with him, could turn her into a notch on his bedpost? Like a fool, she had made his job easy, had thought it was her who'd been doing the pursuing. But all along he'd held her by strings, had kept her at arm's length knowing that would make her want him all the more.

Would make her fall in love.

Her throat grew tight, and her lips turned dry. She had to leave now before she cried.

He stared into her eyes, as though by looking he could read her mind. 'It isn't what you think,' he said fiercely.

Even now, she wanted him, felt the connection between them entrapping her like steel.

He took hold of her arm.

She tried to shake her arm free. 'Let me go,' she demanded, as his hand tightened.

'You're upset,' he said.

She tried to laugh, to show by that action that his words weren't true. 'I'm not upset,' she said, forcing her voice steady. 'I simply have to go. I got what I came for.'

He flinched and gripped her tighter. 'I'm glad we made love.'

'I'm sure you are. You won your bet.'

He blinked, looked confused, then his expression cleared. 'I didn't win,' he said, smiling. 'Did you think I bet Jenny I could make love to you?'

'Didn't you?' she asked coldly. She lifted her chin, tried to dissolve the weight crushing her chest. But perspiration gathered on her brow. She had to get out before she disgraced herself further, before he found out what she didn't want him to know. That he had made her fall in love with him.

'No,' he denied. 'The bet I made with Jenny was not that I could have sex, but that I could do without it.'

Which was why, the night before, Jenny had encouraged her to talk to Jake. His assistant hadn't wanted to tell her she was the focus of a bet.

'Why?' Mel demanded. She should

feel relieved, should be glad of the out, should be feeling anything but this unrelenting pain.

'It doesn't matter why.'

She pulled hard against his grip and yanked her arm free. 'You owe me an answer.'

'It was just a stupid bet.'

'I'm the one who's been stupid.' She rolled off the bed, grabbed her nightie from the floor.

'No, you weren't,' he said fiercely. He, too, rose. 'Where are you going?'

'Anywhere you're not.'

'You can't go,' he insisted.

'Then tell me the truth.'

The moonlight had disappeared, and so had the night. They were standing now in the cold light of day. Jake's face was expressionless. He didn't speak, didn't move. The silence grew so deep, Mel felt she had fallen into a crevice so large all light and truth had vanished.

'I didn't want to make love to you,' he said.

'You calculated that, made a bet about it?'

'I wanted to get to know you, not just make love to you.'

'Why?' she demanded.

'I didn't want to get you pregnant.'

She stared at him, incredulous. 'There's no reason I would. Besides, you told me you wanted to have babies?'

'With the right woman, I do, at the right time.'

He didn't think she was right, or the time was right either. How could she have loved him and got him so wrong? Her head spun, didn't function, couldn't think past the pain. 'It doesn't add up,' she finally said. 'There are ways to prevent pregnancy.'

'Ways that don't always work,' he said, his voice bitter.

'What do you mean?'

He rose from his bed and took a step closer. She could see his eyes now, could see his pain.

'I was seeing a woman before I met

you. She told me she was pregnant.'

'And was she?' Mel asked. Would a cherub with Jake's face appear in a few months? Mel's heart twisted. She didn't want a baby, not now, maybe not ever, but she didn't want anyone else to bear Jake's child.

'No,' he said.

'But you were sorry she wasn't.' Mel fought the knowledge she could see in his eyes.

'No,' he denied, then he gave a slight shrug, the gesture, somehow, the most vulnerable she'd ever seen. 'I didn't want a baby with her. I barely knew her, didn't love her.'

'But you did want a baby.'

'Yes,' he admitted, 'but I wanted a woman first. Not just for sex, but for her mind, her heart.' He stepped forward again.

He was too tall, too big. If he took her in his arms, she wouldn't have the strength to leave.

'And the bet?' she demanded hastily.

'I wanted to get to know a woman

first before I made love to her.'

'So you made a bet with Jenny.'

'She didn't think I could do it.'

'You couldn't. You haven't.' Mel glanced toward the bed where they'd just made love, could still feel the heat sizzling around them. With a shiver of need, she turned back to Jake.

'I got what I wanted,' he said, with a smile. 'I got to know you.' His eyes glowed with a light that seemed to come from within. 'To like you.'

'And a baby?' Mel said quickly, unable to bear any words of love.

'I want that too.'

Her heart felt as though it had shattered. She stepped backwards, opened the door, edged through it before he could react, before he could again cast a death knell on their relationship. With a strength born of fear and a sense of desperation, she ran across the patio and didn't look back.

The back door to the house was open and she fled through it to the kitchen, which, for the first time, was not warmly familiar. The room looked suddenly filled with shadows, seemed to menace with shapes that held no meaning.

She couldn't stay in this place so close to Jake, but couldn't seem either to force her feet forward. She wanted to leave but found no strength to go. She closed the back door and leaned against it, listening for some sound that Jake had followed.

She heard nothing except for the ticking of the clock and the sound of crickets drifting in through the open window. Despair seeped through her.

Jake didn't want her.

Not enough to come after her.

She should be glad, but found no joy in her heart.

13

Jake's glance shied away from Jenny's disapproving frown, but he couldn't shut out the sound of her voice.

'Have you called Mel yet?' his assistant demanded.

'I'm not calling her,' he growled.

'You're an idiot,' she said.

'Don't push it, Jenny.'

'Someone has to make you see sense.'

'There is no sense.'

'You finally find the woman you want and you simply let her walk away.' Jenny leaned on his desk, thrust her face towards his. 'You've got to call her,' she insisted.

'She's not the woman I want.' He pulled out his check book and scribbled madly. 'Here,' he said, 'this is for you.'

She took it, stared down at it, then looked back at him. 'Jake,' she said, her voice more gentle.

'I don't want to talk about it,' he said warningly. 'Now get out of here. I have to work.'

'I'm not going anywhere until you promise to call her.'

'There's no point,' Jake said wearily. He had to stop talking, had to banish Mel from his mind. Impossible, if Jenny brought her up every two minutes.

'Do you want her, or not?'

'What I want doesn't matter.'

Jenny shook her head. 'You always get everything you want. It's one of the things I love about you.'

'Not this time.'

'It's not like you to give up.'

His throat went dry. 'She doesn't want kids.' That thought, as before, broke his heart.

'Even with you?'

'I didn't ask her that.'

'Don't you think you'd better?'

'She made things perfectly plain right from the beginning.' He hesitated. 'She didn't want a relationship. She just wanted sex.'

'Sounds like someone I used to know.' His friend's eyes held no sympathy. 'You managed to change. She will too.'

'I don't think so,' Jake muttered. 'Or she wouldn't have left.' He'd waited long moments for her to return, not wanting to push her, rush her, or scare her.

Like he felt scared. Another thing he hadn't expected. He hadn't anticipated either the rush of sensation when she drew near or the tightening in his chest when he smelled her scent. But most overwhelming of all was when he held her, and his heart began to pound like sticks on drums, without rhythm, without pace, just frantic and hard.

Until he felt as though he couldn't catch his breath.

'She probably wanted you to go after her,' Jenny said, breaking into his thoughts. She gazed at him pityingly. 'Phone her,' she ordered. 'Tell her what you feel.'

'She knows how I feel.'

'Maybe she doesn't.'

Jake pursed his lips. Perhaps Jenny was right. But he couldn't talk to Mel on the phone. If he was going to convince her not to give up on kids, he would have to look her dead in the eye.

* * *

An idea that appealed less the longer he thought about it. He'd been standing outside Jessie's house for ten minutes, hoping against hope that Mel would emerge. He'd phoned her at home but Trish had said she was at Jessie's, would be finishing work around six o'clock. He looked at his watch. It was ten past six now.

Damn the woman. He didn't want to go inside, not with Jessie watching and listening to everything they said. Fond as he'd become of the old lady since he'd met her, he didn't fancy stating his case under her eagle eye. She was liable to tell Mel she didn't need any man.

Look what she'd done to that poor bugger Tom.

Any fool could see that Tom loved Jessie with all his heart, but his love had no effect on the old lady's decision. She'd made up her mind that she didn't need a man, so Tom had been tossed out into the cold.

Which was how he'd felt ever since Mel left. Cold and alone and longing for warmth.

Jake sucked in a breath. Jessie or no Jessie, he and Mel had to talk. He strode up the sidewalk leading to Jessie's door and without hesitation rang the bell.

The door opened, but it wasn't Mel who stood in the doorway.

'It's about time you showed up,' Jessie said crossly. Her wiry body rested heavily on her cane. 'Mel's in the bedroom.' The old lady cast him a shrewd look. 'I assume that it's her you've come here to see.'

'Yes,' Jake said firmly.

'About time,' she said again. 'I

couldn't think what's been keeping you.'

'Did Mel say anything?'

The old lady winked. 'She said you were good in bed.'

Heat warmed Jake's cheeks. He frowned and tried to will it away.

'You see that you treat her right,' Jessie ordered.

'I've always treated her right.'

'The poor thing doesn't know if she's coming or going, you've got her so shook up.'

'Is that what she said?'

Jessie stepped aside and ushered him into the hall. 'She thinks you don't like her.'

'She knows I like her.' More than liked her, loved her. Mel knew that too, although he hadn't actually said the words. Jake's frown deepened. Maybe that's what the matter was. Mel wanted to hear the words. Women always set great store by words.

'Come along then,' Jessie ordered. She turned and led the way down the hall, shuffling in slippers too large for her feet.

'These are Tom's,' she said, catching the direction of Jake's glance. 'If he wants them back, he's going to have to come and ask for them.'

'Why did you keep them?'

Jessie's back was to him, but he could tell how she felt as easily as if she faced him. Her back straightened and stiffened and the hand gripping the cane turned white at the knuckles. 'I gave them to him,' her voice rasped out. 'He shouldn't have left them behind.'

'Are you talking to me?' asked Mel in a muffled voice from behind the closed bedroom door.

'You've got a visitor,' Jessie said. She pushed the door open then stepped aside.

Mel stood by the dresser, a dusting cloth in her hand. Jake wanted to go to her, but Jessie's bed was between them. The old woman nudged his back and he stepped forward. Behind him Jessie pulled the door shut.

Mel's eyes grew wide and very blue, and her black hair framed a suddenly pale face. 'What do you want?'

'We need to talk,' Jake said firmly.

'We've talked enough.' Turning away from him, she picked up Jessie's hand mirror and, for a long moment, stared at her own reflection. Then with a sigh, she ran her cloth over the silver back. 'There's nothing more to say.'

'I haven't told you how I feel about you.'

She faced him again, her eyes growing wider.

He glanced at the bed between them, at the muted colors of the quilt. An old-fashioned quilt like the one on Mel's bed. Only Jessie wasn't old-fashioned and neither was Mel. Not when it came to sex, hopes and dreams.

He stepped around the bed, needing Mel's touch, needing the connection he felt when she was with him. She moved backwards towards the window as though to keep some distance between them.

He took another step and touched her arm, was unprepared for the jolt that gripped his heart. 'I'm in love with you,' he said.

Her arm burned where he touched her, but his words seared her more, and a pain began that no words could cure. 'It's not me you want,' she accused. 'What you want is a baby.'

'You're right,' he said, 'about wanting the baby. But there's only one woman I want as its mother.' He stared into her eyes. 'That woman is you.'

The air seemed to stop as it passed between Mel's lips. With a great effort, she sucked it through. 'Go home, Jake,' she said, wearily. 'There's nothing here for you.'

His hand swept her arm and settled on her waist. Butterflies fluttered and swarmed through her belly making her want and not want all at once.

She glanced at his hand, tried to brush it away, tried to stop his power by banishing him from her.

He lifted his hand to touch her

cheek. 'Do you love me?' he asked.

He could never know how much. She had to keep that secret hidden, for with a single touch, Jake could turn her emotions inside out.

'It's no good,' she said. 'You know what I want.'

'Sex,' he answered. 'I'm all for that, too.'

Her medical texts had made sex sound simple, but those books didn't know the power of Jake. A power which now she couldn't allow him to exert. She willed all sensation to cease where he touched.

'Sex, Jake,' she said softly, 'not love.'

'They can go hand in hand.'

'Not with me, they can't.' Not if she wanted to be a surgeon. His hand drifted to her face, creating warmth there, and beneath his fingers her pulse pounded fiercely.

'You want me,' he whispered, 'as much as I want you.'

'I've never denied wanting you.'

'No,' he agreed. 'You threw yourself

258

at me.' He swept her hair back from her face.

This time she found the strength to push his hand away, but as she did so, her fingers betrayed her and drifted out to touch his chest.

'This has got to end,' she told him hoarsely.

'It's only beginning.'

'I've got years of study ahead.'

'Study isn't everything.'

She swallowed hard. 'It is to me.'

'But to be part of a family . . . you can do both.'

'I can't,' she said. 'It's not possible.'

Her words were like arrows that found their marks, for Jake's face turned pale and his fingers curled into fists. But however much her statement seemed to have hurt Jake, a searing sorrow ripped Mel's own chest.

She had tried to expunge the love engulfing her soul from the very first moment she'd recognized its presence. She'd fled Jake's bed, tried to banish his image, had tried not to feel what he made her feel. But nothing had worked. She did love this man, despite the fact that it wasn't truly her that he wanted, but rather a vehicle to obtain a child.

He opened his mouth.

She turned away.

He began to speak but his words were drowned by a thump from the hall outside.

'Jessie,' Mel called, pushing past Jake. She ran for the door when all she wanted was his arms. Dread built in her chest, grew swiftly to panic.

She opened the door and found Jessie sprawled in an unnatural way across the hall. Her legs were splayed and her head was propped at an angle that surely must hurt. Her eyes were shut and her complexion was white, and when Mel touched her hand, she found it clammy.

'Call an ambulance,' Mel cried over her shoulder to Jake, then she crouched by her friend, tears flooding her eyes. She swiped them away and took hold of Jessie's wrist, feeling for a pulse that was barely there.

It faded in and out, beating in syncopation like a reggae drum. Her breath, too, when Mel dropped her head to Jessie's mouth, seemed as non-existent as a breeze in the doldrums.

Mel turned to Jake, gathered strength from his presence. He'd already pulled his phone from his pocket and was spitting out Jessie's address to the emergency operator.

'She's barely breathing,' Mel said, sucking in air, wishing her air could go into Jessie as easily. For an instant her sight seemed to swim with black dots as panic expanded and swirled inside, then taking a deep breath, she lowered her head and blew air through Jessie's lips.

She counted between breaths, tried to believe her efforts useful, but at first there seemed to be no response. No flutter of air back out through the lips, no increase of color on Jessie's pale face. Then just as her fear was ready to explode out, Mel saw the faint rise and fall of Jessie's chest.

Relief seared her heart, followed swiftly by fear. Jessie might be breathing, but she remained unconscious, and the color of her skin was not any better. Mel took hold of Jessie's hand, willing her to know she was not alone. Then she glanced at Jake.

The reassurance in his eyes steadied her. He touched Mel's shoulder, the gesture light but enough to push back the fear.

'I'll get a blanket,' he said, and disappeared into the bedroom. He emerged a moment later with a quilt and pillow. He swiftly tucked the quilt around Jessie's body then maneuvered the pillow under her head.

Strong hands, yet gentle, hands that could keep an old woman safe, or a baby . . . or a lover.

Somewhere in the distance, Mel could hear a siren, screaming out as though voicing her fear. She prayed it would get there faster, would save this woman she loved as family.

Jake touched her again, this time on her hand, enclosing her fingers with his own. He took hold also of Jessie's other hand and completed a circle of solidarity between them, making Mel feel that nothing bad could happen, not with Jake connecting them all.

'She'll be all right,' he said firmly. 'You've helped her be all right.'

Mel shut her eyes and tried to believe him, tried to banish the image of her grandmother dying. *Her* breathing had stopped just when they thought it would begin again, *her* heart unable to keep on beating. She couldn't bear it if the same thing happened to Jessie.

Jake released Mel's hand and draped an arm around her shoulders. 'You've kept her going. You have to believe she'll be all right.'

A pounding on the door drowned more speech, and Jake leaped up to let the paramedics in. It took only moments for them to bundle Jessie up on to a stretcher and out the door.

Only moments, but it seemed a

lifetime to Mel. She found herself shivering and couldn't seem to stop. The only place she was warm was where Jake touched her.

'I want to go with her,' she said hoarsely.

'We'll both go,' Jake replied. 'I'll take you in my car.'

'No,' she said, 'I'll go in the ambulance.' She wanted nothing more than to stay with Jake, to soak up his comfort and bathe in his strength, but the longer she allowed herself to be near him, the harder it would be to pull away.

Jake touched Mel's elbow, his eyes filled with worry. 'You've done what you can. Let me take care of you.'

Mel's body sagged. 'Jess needs me,' she said, with a shuddering breath. 'I have to go with her.'

Jake's eyes darkened, but he nodded in assent, then walked with Mel down the stairs and out to the driveway toward the open door of the ambulance.

For what seemed the first time in a blistering hot summer, the skies had opened and rain poured down. The drops mingled with the tears Mel couldn't keep in, and the fear inside grew larger than space.

'It'll be all right,' Jake said again, draping his arms around her shoulders.

The wipers swished the rain off the ambulance windows, but as fast as they cleared other drops took their place. As tears took the place of the ones Mel removed.

For an instant, she laid her cheek on Jake's shirt then, with a wrench, she pulled away. She climbed into the ambulance and sat next to Jessie, watching Jake as the vehicle drove off. He stood legs apart and his body strong. She clung to the sight as long as she could, then, with a sigh, turned back to Jessie and took the old woman's hand in her own.

14

Mel stared at the form of Jessie in the bed, looking much smaller than she did standing up. The shape of her body was barely discernible draped as it was in white cotton sheets.

Thank heavens they had transferred her up onto the ward away from the confusion of the emergency room, where doctors and nurses pulled curtains around patients, creating a terrifying sense of things gone wrong.

If only Jake were here. Where on earth could he be?

This waiting was hard, as was the non-information, and the frustrating helplessness of nothing to do. The only thing she knew was that Jessie had suffered a heart attack and that she'd been lucky Mel and Jake had been there.

Mel took a deep breath, focused

again on Jessie, tried to count the seconds between her in and out breaths. They at least seemed more regular, were visible now, could be heard in the air hissing through her lips.

Mel wrapped her arms around her body, tried to banish the chill that shook her still. It must be a reaction to Jessie's collapse or to the diagnosis of her friend's heart attack. If only Jake were there to hold her in his arms. She knew that she would feel better then.

Where was he? she wondered. Why didn't he come?

A doctor came in and joined the intern who was bending over Jessie, a stethoscope to his ear. Together they held a whispered consultation, glancing first at the chart the intern held, then at the screen above Jessie's bed.

Mel shivered again and wished that this was over, that Jessie was at home in her comfortable bed, not stuck in a hospital with tubes crossing her body and instruments beeping in her ear.

The doctor turned at last, looked at

Mel in her corner, and before she could prepare for what he might say, he strode towards her and stopped in front.

'You're not family,' he said, with a frown.

'Jessie has no family,' Mel whispered in reply.

'She's had a heart attack,' he said baldly.

'I know,' Mel replied. 'That's what they said downstairs.'

'It's serious, I'm afraid.'

The chill permeating Mel's body settled deep in her gut. 'How serious?' she asked.

'We'll have to operate.'

'When?'

'As soon as a theatre comes free.'

They were meant to operate on Jessie in September, but not on her heart, not an operation of a life and death sort.

'Isn't there some sort of procedure about these things?' Mel asked. 'Permission forms — '

'That's all been taken care of.'

'By whom?'

The doctor consulted his chart. 'Her lawyer apparently.'

Jake. Jake was here.

'He also arranged that she be brought up here.' The doctor turned away, his attention demanded by a nurse who had just arrived and had in her hand a new batch of forms.

So Jake was responsible for things moving so swiftly, for getting Jessie from the emergency ward to a private room. It also explained where Jake had been, what he'd been doing while she watched Jessie breathe.

'How's she doing?' a voice suddenly whispered from behind.

Mel spun around. 'Jake!' She longed to fly into his arms, had to struggle not to cry. 'They want to operate.'

'I know,' Jake replied, reaching out to touch her. 'It'll be a good thing.'

Suddenly the monitor over Jessie's bed rang. The strident sound shot fear through Mel's heart. With the speed of sound, medical staff arrived, and clustered around Jessie doing God knew what.

Mel caught her breath, but that was all the time it took for them to wheel Jessie away. The only sign left that she'd once been there was the space where her bed had been. Mel swallowed hard, tried to stop the moan pushing past her throat.

'She'll be all right,' Jake repeated, pulling her to him. 'They'll do a bypass and she'll be all right.'

For a moment she let herself sink into his comfort, let his man's strength bolster her own. Then with a soul- and heart-wrenching motion, she shrugged away from his embrace. Jake's heat and scent still engulfed her, still gave her the comfort her body craved. But she couldn't give in, couldn't let herself go, couldn't wrap herself in the care and love of the man. For if she did it would be harder on Jake.

He wanted children, a wife, and a home. She wanted to be a doctor. She couldn't do both.

Air entered her body in shallow gasps. She couldn't meet Jake's eyes,

270

had to look away. If she saw in the flesh what she was giving up, she knew that she could never do it.

'I'm going to Jessie's,' she told him swiftly. 'She's going to want a few of her things.'

'Time enough for that later.'

'I want to get them now.'

'I'll take you,' he offered.

'Please stay here. If anything happens — ' She fought tears from her voice. 'Someone has to be here.'

'That someone should be you.'

Numbly, she shook her head. 'I have to go.' And she had to do it now before she lost her resolve.

With no final glance in Jake's direction, Mel strode to the door and walked right through. By keeping her gaze fixed on the floor in front, she was able to navigate the hall. It was only once she was in the elevator that she began to shake with fear, with sorrow, and with gut-wrenching regret.

* * *

271

Mel glanced at her watch and pushed her cup aside, not caring that cold tea slopped over the rim. She hadn't left, hadn't been able to, not until she knew that Jessie was all right. She'd holed up in the cafeteria, had been fearful the whole time that Jake would show up and her resolve to keep her distance would be lost.

She'd have to face him now, have to face her need, for according to the nurse when she'd called up to the ward, Jessie had made it through her operation and would soon be back in her room recovering.

The elevator on the ride up was packed with a family talking excitedly about the new baby they were there to see. Mel shut her eyes and wished that she could block her ears. She didn't want to hear about what she couldn't have. At least not now. Not for years.

Which wouldn't work for Jake. He wanted a baby now. She couldn't ask him to wait.

The hall, when she got out, hadn't seemed so long before, or maybe it was that her steps had somehow slowed. Her chest felt tight as though it couldn't take the air that her lungs insisted on pulling in.

322, 324 . . . Jessie was in 326. Her door was partially shut.

Mel stared at the handle for a long moment, then pressing her lips tight, put out her hand and opened it further. Her gaze flew to the bed, and to the man standing by Jessie.

'Tom,' she whispered. Jessie's Tom. He was holding Jessie's hand as though he never intended to let it go.

Jessie, for her part, gazed weakly up at her former lover, her face white and frail, but her eyes filled with love.

The tension building in Mel's body exploded outward in a rush. Tears poured down her face, blurring her vision. She almost didn't see Jake standing in the corner.

Jake, too, was gazing at Tom and Jessie and from the smile on his face he had probably brought about this wonder also.

The knot in Mel's belly re-tangled and grew tighter, and she turned away before anyone could see her. Now that she knew her friend was safe, and had beside her a man who loved her, she didn't want to stay and face Jake. Not when her own heart was filled with despair for the loss of love and the family she'd never have.

She fled down the hall the way she had come, then down another hall, then another. The corridors seemed built like a maze in a box, each one turning into the next.

With unseeing eyes, she fled and prayed that the speed would release the longing that gripped her. Whenever she thought of Jake or his warmth, she didn't know how she could lose him from her life.

She finally stopped when she could go no further. Breathing hard, she stared through the glass before her. Rows of babies of every shape, size and color lay side by side. Tiny ones, bigger, blond- and black-haired, they lay in their cots, their little hands waving. As though they knew that beyond the window their relatives and friends longed for a gesture.

A sturdy baby in the second row gazed with bright eyes in Mel's direction. She'd read somewhere that newborn babies couldn't see anything other than shape and shadow, but this baby seemed to focus with wise, crinkled eyes on a stranger that needed him more than she'd known.

He looked like Jake, this baby in his cot, had Jake's dark hair and decisive gaze. He, too, had the ability to lurch Mel's heart and make her legs go weak at the knees.

She loved Jake. She knew it. He must know it, too. And she wanted a baby. She knew that now also. A darling baby who looked just like Jake.

Why then was she running away?

Jessie had run, but had come back to Tom, had obviously needed him as much as he did her.

But wanting to love didn't offer solutions to the problem that still seemed overwhelming. Wanting to love didn't make four years of medical training magically disappear. Plus two years more if she went into surgery.

Although she was becoming less and less sure about becoming a surgeon. Since starting work with Jess, she'd grown to love the old woman, loved her spunk, her strength, and the wisdom she'd spent a lifetime acquiring. Other old people she'd met through her job also had much to offer the world still.

Together with young families, she could have a general practice, could experience new beginnings and dignified endings, could enjoy the entire cycle of living.

To be a general practitioner was a route she knew she could enjoy. But children . . . what about children? Jake wanted them *now*. With four years of medical school before her, how could she ever offer him that?

'Mel,' a voice behind her said softly.

Before she could turn, she felt two hands on her waist, and then they moved higher and encircled her chest. Holding her, rocking her, thrilling and uplifting her, bowling her over with a feeling of love.

'I was worried,' Jake whispered.

'About Jessie?' she asked.

'Jessie's fine.'

She turned to face him.

'I was worried about you.'

'I'm fine, too.' Or she would be if the tension gripping her mind and spirit would disappear and set her free. If only she could relax against her lover's broad chest.

'You don't look fine.' His gaze held hers. 'Why did you run from Jessie's room?'

'I saw Tom,' she lied.

Jake's eyes searched hers. 'I called Tom.'

'I thought perhaps you had.'

'Jessie loved him,' he went on. 'She needed him near.'

'How did you know? She never said that to me.'

Jake shrugged. 'She didn't have to say it.'

Mel lifted one brow. 'Men's intuition?'

'If you like.' He chuckled. 'The easier answer is that it was there in her voice.'

'I didn't think men were adept at reading tones.'

He chuckled again, and the sound warmed her heart. She wanted to keep talking, to enjoy being with him, for then she wouldn't think of problems with no solutions.

'I'm a lawyer,' he went on. 'I spend my life reading tones.' His gaze held hers. 'And finding solutions where no solutions seem possible.'

His eyes drew her to him, seemed to offer light and a path through the maze that encircled her emotions.

'What sort of solutions?' she asked, her voice cracking.

'The sort that make you happy.' He pulled her closer. 'But I still want to know why you ran?'

'I was worried.' Her throat closed. She swallowed, began again. 'When I saw Jessie was all right, I felt so relieved.'

'Not usually a reason to run away.'

'She had Tom. She looked happy.'

'But?' he asked.

'I saw you.' Her pulse thudded against her temples.

'Seeing me made you run?'

She couldn't think when he looked at her as he did now, as though he meant to kiss her and never let her go.

'Not quite the reaction I would like,' he murmured.

'I was afraid,' she admitted.

'Of me?' he asked again.

'Of how I feel,' she replied.

'How do you feel?' His voice had dropped to just above a whisper and his lips were so near she could feel their vibration.

'As though we have to stop seeing each other.'

'You don't mean that,' he said, not drawing back.

His lips were so close, she could reach out and kiss him, could lose herself in the magic of their touch.

'You love me,' he said.

'What makes you think so?'

'I can tell,' he assured her. 'Just like I love you.'

The fact that Jake loved her didn't solve a thing, just made the pain of denial that much harder.

'You love me,' he said again, not stating it as a question, but as a verifiable fact obvious to all. She knew then he had no trouble reading the love in her eyes.

She pulled her gaze from his.

'Or is it just lust?' This time it was a question, one uttered in a drawling, teasing voice.

'Definitely partly lust,' she answered shakily.

'Just partly?' he demanded, his hand brushing her breast.

Her nipples tightened in response. She glanced around to see if anyone was looking, but for a rare moment, there was no one else there.

'I can't think when you do that,' she protested.

'Didn't you once tell me,' he said, smiling, 'that we thought too much?'

'I don't know. You're making it difficult to remember.'

'Good,' he said, drawing a finger up her throat to her mouth. 'There's no need to remember. Just look to the future.'

'There is no future.' The thought made her want to cry. 'At least not for us.'

'You are my future.'

She stared into his eyes, longed to believe him, longed to know that his vision was possible for her. 'But you want children,' she said, 'and a wife that is home. I can't do that.' She cast a longing glance toward the babies behind the glass.

'I'm not asking you to.'

'So what are you asking? That I be your mistress?'

'Sounds good,' he said throatily. 'But

I think that we can do better than that.'

'Jake, I want — '

'What is it that you want?'

'I want you,' she said honestly.

'But you want to be a doctor too?'

Numbly, she nodded.

'The two aren't mutually exclusive.' He drew his fingers across her lips.

'They are when you throw babies into the mix.' The desire to have his child assailed her again, ripped at her heart like a wild beast with its prey. 'I have changed my mind about one thing, though. I've decided not to become a surgeon.' That decision must have been waiting in her heart to emerge, for when she'd seen the babies in the nursery she'd known she wanted to work with them too.

'I don't want you giving up your dreams for me.'

'You are my dream.' She examined his lips, remembered how they'd felt pressed against hers. 'A different sort of dream.'

'I want to be your life.' He smiled

down at her. 'Not all of it though. You'll have to fit in all the patients. You'll have babies, adults, and the elderly like Jessie.' He kissed her lightly on the lips then captured her breath with a long, slow kiss. 'You'll be a wonderful doctor,' he said, holding her tight. 'Just as you'll be a wonderful wife.'

'But how — '

'If you're not a surgeon, your training will be shorter.'

She nodded, shrugging helplessly as she again thought through the math. 'Not much less.'

'I want you, Mel.'

'I want you, too!'

'We don't need children — '

'I can't let you give them up.'

'I'm thirty-two, not over the hill! I'm saying yes, I want a baby, but I'm prepared to wait.' He kissed her again. 'If what I'm waiting for is you and a baby that's ours.'

Mel felt as though her heart was growing, pushing out the ache lodged in her chest. Love overwhelmed her for the man before her. 'It'll still take years.'

'Years that we'll enjoy together.' He nuzzled her ear, sparking a heat that soared through every vein.

'I'll have to spend hours every day studying.'

'Not all the hours.' He dropped kisses across her temple, dragged heat in their wake.

'We can't do this here.' But she pulled him closer. His body melted into hers, made a promise no words could match.

'We could practice making babies,' Jake suggested.

She laughed out loud. 'I don't think you need the practice. I, on the other hand . . . '

She couldn't finish her sentence, not when his lips locked on to hers. When she emerged at last from the kiss they shared, she pulled away and stared into his eyes. 'Are you sure, Jake?' she asked.

He smiled and his happiness showed in his eyes, together with the resolve she'd seen in them before. 'I'm sure I want you as my wife — ' His voice was steady and assured. ' — as the mother of my babies, and my lover for life.'

'A lifetime's a long time.'

'Not so long when it's shared.'

She imagined sharing her life with this man who'd been a stranger, and knew she'd been imagining it from the moment they first met. Mel swept her fingers through his hair dreamily. 'Trish is going to want to take credit for this, you know!'

'She's welcome to it.' He gazed at her curiously. 'But what did Trish do?'

'She told me to go for it,' Mel answered, with a grin. 'I'm not sure she thought I could pull it off.'

'What, sex?' Jake asked grinning. 'Or snagging an eligible bachelor like me?'

'You did all the snagging,' Mel countered indignantly.

Jake laughed, and held her tighter. 'I wonder what your cousin Tony will say? He warned me off, you know.'

'Tony thinks you're great. It's my

father you should be worrying about.'
Mel chuckled as Jake drew back, his
brows joining above his nose in a frown.
'He's very protective of his only child.
But if you can develop an interest in his
tomatoes, you might just stand a
fighting chance.'

'I can like tomatoes.' He grinned.
'Especially if you turn them into that
spaghetti sauce you're always bragging
about.'

She lowered her lashes, gave him her
best sexy look. 'I hear spaghetti sauce is
especially delicious when licked off the
skin.'

He laughed out loud and pulled her
to him again, then kissed her so
thoroughly her head began to spin.
She'd offered her body. He'd taken her
heart. And now she was giving him her
soul in return.

She'd wanted him.
He'd taken her.
She was his.

We do hope that you have enjoyed reading this large print book.

Did you know that all of our titles are available for purchase?

We publish a wide range of high quality large print books including:
Romances, Mysteries, Classics
General Fiction
Non Fiction and Westerns

Special interest titles available in large print are:
The Little Oxford Dictionary
Music Book, Song Book
Hymn Book, Service Book

Also available from us courtesy of Oxford University Press:
Young Readers' Dictionary
(large print edition)
Young Readers' Thesaurus
(large print edition)

For further information or a free brochure, please contact us at:
Ulverscroft Large Print Books Ltd.,
The Green, Bradgate Road, Anstey,
Leicester, LE7 7FU, England.
Tel: (00 44) **0116 236 4325**
Fax: (00 44) **0116 234 0205**

Other titles in the
Linford Romance Library:

THE FERRYBOAT

Kate Blackadder

When Judy and Tom Jeffrey are asked by their daughter Holly and her Scottish chef husband Corin if they will join them in buying the Ferryboat Hotel in the West Highlands, they take the plunge and move north. The rundown hotel needs much expensive upgrading, and what with local opposition to some of their plans — and worrying about their younger daughter, left down south with her flighty grandma — Judy begins to wonder if they've made a terrible mistake . . .